The Wedding

A GORGEOUSLY UPLIFTING AND
HEARTWARMING ROMANCE

RACHEL GRIFFITHS

COSY COTTAGE BOOKS

For my family, with love always. XXX

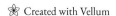

The Wedding

You never forget your first love...

When teacher Chloe Redgrave receives a text message out of the blue from her childhood best friend, she's plunged into turmoil. Willow Treharne is getting married in the Cornish village where they grew up and she wants Chloe to be her bridesmaid. The catch? They haven't seen each other in years.

Willow hopes she's done the right thing inviting Chloe to her wedding but after what happened more than a decade ago, she can't be sure. However, she has a reason for wanting Chloe to be there and that overrides her doubts and concerns.

Surfer Theo Treharne is happy for his sister but also anxious about seeing Chloe. After all, they didn't exactly part on good terms. Will he be able to stay calm when he sees the woman who broke his heart again?

As family and friends gather in the beautiful Cornish village for the romantic clifftop wedding, will there be smiles and laughter, or will the past prove to be too difficult to forget?

Chloe

'Pardon?' Chloe Redgrave dragged her gaze from her smartphone and blinked at the woman sitting opposite her in the staffroom.

'I asked if everything's all right,' the woman – Jane, she thought her name was – replied. 'Your face blanched when you looked at your phone.'

'Oh... uh...' Chloe glanced at her phone then back at Jane. 'Yes... just an unexpected message from an old friend.'

Jane smiled. 'Nothing like a blast from the past to unsettle you of a morning. Fancy another coffee?' She pointed at Chloe's mug that sat empty on the low table in front of her.

'Yes, please. That would be lovely.'

As Jane walked away, Chloe tried to swallow but her mouth had gone dry, so she reluctantly put her phone down, pulled a bottle of water from her bag and took a sip. Her childhood friend, Willow Treharne, had sent her a message inviting her to her wedding. But... not just inviting her as a guest... *as a brides-maid*. She took another sip of water, momentarily wishing it was something stronger, then put the bottle back in her bag, her mind whirling with thoughts.

'Here you go.' Jane set Chloe's mug down on the table. 'I didn't add sugar though... forgot to ask if you like it.'

'No, that's great, thanks.'

'Sweet enough.' Jane chuckled at her own joke. 'Very wise to have your name on your mug. I can't count the number of mugs I've lost over the years in different schools. Hazard of being a supply teacher I guess.'

Chloe nodded at Jane. 'It is, right? Mind you, even when I was permanent at a school, I still lost mugs. If your name isn't on it, it seems that a mug is fair game.'

Jane settled into the chair opposite Chloe and stretched out her long slim legs clad in smart black trousers. 'Have you been at this school long?'

Chloe gave a brief shake of her head. 'I work with a supply agency and when I signed with them, I said I'd prefer short term placements, so I rarely work at the same school for more than a few days at a time.'

'I'd love a permanent contract.' Jane cradled her mug between her hands as if she was cold and gazed out of the window dreamily. 'It's exhausting going from school to school but finding a permanent job as an art teacher at my age isn't easy.'

Chloe picked up her coffee and took a sip to buy some time before responding. She'd found that announcing that she'd walked away from a permanent job to supply teachers desperate for such a position didn't go down well. 'I'm kind of enjoying the... freedom of working at different schools right now. I might want to settle somewhere in the future... but for now, I'm good.'

Jane raised her over-plucked eyebrows. 'That's nice for you... but you're still young. I'm fifty-five and a lot of head teachers want the young and newly qualified teachers, and won't give anyone over thirty the time of day. I came into teaching in my forties.' She placed a hand on her chest and took a deep breath as if preparing herself for what she was about to divulge. 'A bitter divorce left me yearning for a career change and teaching seemed like the right one. However... I haven't been able to get a permanent job. I don't mind supply work but I can't imagine moving around so much when I'm sixty-five.'

'You still imagine teaching in your sixties?' Chloe's eyes widened.

'Of course.' Jane knitted her brows. 'I had to start over after my divorce and I need the salary. Don't we all have to work until we drop these days?'

Chloe sipped her coffee, swallowing her dismay at Jane's outlook. Who wanted to work until they dropped? The idea was terrifying. Yes, she'd had a permanent job in a fairly good school and then another one, almost like she was trying them on for fit, but despite her best efforts, neither school had felt right. Her heart just hadn't been in it the same way some of her colleagues' had seemed to be, so she'd resigned and gone on supply. Before handing in her notice at the second school, she'd told herself that lots of people didn't work their dream jobs and that in the current economic climate, any job was a great job, but she'd also felt guilty because there could be some enthusiastic teacher out there – like Jane – who was desperate for a job. In a way, Chloe had felt like she was job blocking, so she'd summoned her courage and quit. And she hadn't had one regret in the past year. Supply wasn't great in some ways – you didn't get to know the pupils well and you didn't have the benefits that a permanent job offered – but you also had freedoms that you wouldn't have in a permanent job. As with everything, there were pros and cons. And the lack of pressure from not having marking, report deadlines and repeated lesson observations meant that Chloe was free to focus on other things – like her writing. The only problem was that so far, she'd been too tired from driving around to different schools and from day-to-day life that she hadn't got round to writing. She had ideas and plans, agents and publishers she'd like to approach, but it was something she hadn't done.

Yet...

As long as she kept telling herself that she'd do it one day, she had hope. But some days she did wonder what exactly was holding her back. Was it really tiredness and lack of time? Or was it fear of rejection and of failure? Because if she failed at writing then what else could she do?

Chloe jumped as the tinny buzzer vibrated through the air signalling the end of break. Opposite her, Jane gulped the rest of her coffee, wiped her mug with a tissue then stuffed it into her bag. 'Right then...' she said as she stood up. 'I'm teaching Year 8 how to draw hands this lesson. Have a good one and I'll see you at lunch, shall I?'

'Sure.' Chloe flashed a smile at Jane then finished her own coffee. She had a group of Year 10 boys next for creative writing and knew exactly how it would pan out. There would be moans and groans (about how they had no ideas and about how much they hated writing stories) until Chloe raised the topic of stories in the music they listened to, the movies they watched and the computer games they all played. They would think for a bit, discuss what she'd said, then their attitudes would shift. Not entirely, no, because it took a while, but once they realised that they were surrounded by stories every day, and that they could find inspiration from the world around them, they didn't feel so threatened by a blank page. If she had longer with them, Chloe would work on this for a few weeks, building their confidence so they felt ready to write and then, hopefully, to share what they'd written. She'd been good at teaching creative writing, she knew that, but it just wasn't enough for her. There were so many aspects of the job that didn't work for her and so she had decided to follow her heart and become an author.

One day soon...

But for now, she had a class of teenagers to inspire, and if she could do that in an hour then she'd be a superhero. Chloe didn't see herself as a superhero at all but she had teaching experience, so she'd do her best.

She slipped her mug in her bag, picked up her phone and left the staffroom, putting Willow's text message from her mind for the next hour at least. There would be time to wonder about why

4

she'd been asked to be a bridesmaid later on when she had an ice-cold glass of white wine in her hand, the windows of her small flat open to let in the early June air, and the weekend weekend stretching out ahead of her.

Willow

~∽∽⌒

'This one's good,' Daniel said, pointing at the lemon cake.

Willow frowned. 'It's OK, but I think I prefer the vanilla sponge.'

'We can have whichever one you prefer, my gorgeous fiancée.' Daniel slid his arm around her shoulders and kissed the top of her head. Willow relaxed against him, marvelling as she always did at how her body responded to him. At six-foot-two and just over eighteen stone, Daniel was like a wall of muscle that dwarfed her five-foot-two-inch frame, but he made her feel so safe and loved that the difference in their height and weight was immaterial. Since falling for Daniel at university where they both studied law, Willow had come to believe that love conquered all.

'Well, I like vanilla sponge... but I know that Mum and Dad like chocolate cake and—'

Daniel turned her to face him, placed a hand under her chin and tilted it so she was looking into his brown eyes. 'Willow... who's getting married?'

She sighed. 'Us.'

'That's right. Not your parents or my parents, not your friends... not right now at least. This is our wedding, so we should have whatever cake we want.' He kissed her softly then dropped his hand from her chin and entwined his fingers with hers as they looked back at the table of cakes.

'Sorry to interrupt...' Mariella, the cake shop owner, had appeared at Willow's side. 'I couldn't help overhearing your discussion and this is a more common problem than you'd imagine. We can, if you like, make a tiered cake with different flavours, or three or four separate cakes on separate stands or... have stands of different flavoured cupcakes. There are so many options available and I'm always open to suggestions if you have any.'

'Oh.' Willow raised her eyebrows. 'Well, that would be a nice idea, wouldn't it, Dan?'

'Which one?' He laughed softly.

'The different cakes on separate stands perhaps?'

'I can see how that would work.' He nodded. 'That way there's something for everyone and you don't fret about who's not happy with what's on offer.'

'Exactly.' Willow smiled.

'We can even do one cake gluten free, dairy free, nut free... whatever works for you and your guests.' Mariella gestured at the range on the table.

'That's fabulous, thank you. If you could make one of the cakes gluten, nut and dairy free, that would be brilliant because one of my friends is allergic to just about everything.'

'We can do that,' Mariella said. 'Right... I'll leave you in peace to finish sampling the cakes and when you're done, you can let me know your thoughts.'

'Thank you.'

Mariella walked away and Willow eyed the cakes, imagining how they would look on her wedding day.

'You always think about everyone else.' Daniel's voice was gruff, and when Willow looked at him, his eyes were shining. For such a big man, he had a soft heart and it was one of the things Willow loved about him. 'I can't believe how lucky I am that I get to marry you.'

'I'm the lucky one,' Willow said as she squeezed his hand. 'The day I met you was the best day of my life.'

'Mine too.' Daniel rubbed his free hand over his eyes. 'Crikey... If I'm this emotional now I'm going to be a wreck on our wedding day.'

'Yeah you will. But I'll be there to hold your hand.' Willow giggled.

'Yeah you will.' Daniel raised her hand and kissed it, and Willow sent out a silent thank you to the universe for sending this wonderful man her way over fourteen years ago.

Chloe

~∞∽

Lying propped up on pillows in bed on a sunny Sunday morning with the bedroom window open to let in the fresh morning air, Chloe sipped her tea. She'd been awake since dawn, disturbed by a dream in which she'd been running along a beach being chased by polar bear. Why a polar bear, she had no idea but she had been – quite rightly – terrified, and when she'd woken her heart had been racing, her sheets wrapped around her legs. The dream had lingered when she'd tried to drop back off, so she'd given up by six-thirty and got up to make a cup of tea.

Just over two weeks had passed since Willow's text message. It hadn't been a long message, just stated that Willow was marrying her partner, Daniel Fashanu, the last Saturday in July and that she'd like to have her old friend Chloe as a bridesmaid. Willow had briefly apologised for the short notice but told Chloe that her maternal grandmother, Barbara Rees, was frail, and they had decided to bring their wedding forwards a year so that Barbara could attend. Chloe knew that lawyers Willow and Daniel had got engaged at Christmas because she'd seen the Facebook post and congratulated them. They made a gorgeous couple, petite Willow with her porcelain complexion, jet black hair and emerald eyes, and tall, muscular Daniel with his broad shoulders, short afro hair and chocolate brown eyes.

Willow and Daniel had met and fallen in love at university and now worked for the same law firm in Sea Breeze Sands, the village where Chloe and Willow had grown up. The village Willow had returned to with her partner, keen to settle down there. The village Chloe had fled all those years ago and only returned to in order to visit her family.

Sea Breeze Sands was a beautiful location on the north coast of Cornwall, an equal distance from Newquay and St Ives with a beach nestled in a picturesque cove. It was popular with tourists in the summer months and with surfers all year round. Chloe had thought she'd never want to leave as a child, but then she'd grown up and her mind had changed. Things had happened and she'd dreamt of living in a city, of being a successful author, of living a different life. Her dreams hadn't exactly worked out as she'd planned, but even so, returning to Sea Breeze Sands had not been on her agenda for the summer, except for a few fleeting visits to see her mum and gran. However, if she accepted Willow's invite, she'd need to return sooner than planned and to stay for longer. And there was the risk of bumping into people she'd prefer not to see. The *one person* she'd prefer not to see. Of having to spend an extended amount of time in the company of that person.

But Willow and Chloe went back a long way and if she didn't go, wouldn't she always wonder if she'd done the right thing? A lot of time had passed since Chloe had left Sea Breeze Sands for good. Perhaps everyone else had moved on, just like Chloe had.

Or like she told herself she had.

She swiped the screen of her phone and read the message from Willow again. She should have replied before now but she hadn't known what to say. It was time to swallow her fears and her pride and act like a grown up. After all, she couldn't stay away forever, and this was the perfect reason to pin her knickers to her vest and head on home.

Wasn't it?

Theo

Theo turned the sign on the door to 'open' then returned to the counter and picked up his phone. He flicked through the apps to find the music one then selected a playlist and connected to the Wi-Fi. The family surf shop was filled with an uplifting pop song and he smiled, grateful for the comfort that music offered, even when times were tough.

Not that Theo's life was usually tough, but lately he'd been feeling a bit low for a few reasons. The first was because his sister, Willow, was getting married. He was delighted for her, she was very happy with Daniel and they seemed made for each other, but it had reminded him that he was thirty-five and still single. Not exactly over the hill, of course, and he wasn't exactly desperate to have someone in his life, but sometimes it would have been nice to have the comfort of a relationship, a special someone to love him in return. He'd had that once, a long time ago, but since then love had eluded him. He'd had brief relationships with some lovely women, but he'd been ruined for all of them by his first serious relationship, finding himself unable to commit because none of the women were who he wanted them to be. He'd done his best not to hurt anyone, it was why he got out early before emotions became serious. His sister told him that he didn't give any of the women a chance to matter to him, but she didn't understand how it felt to love deeply then lose that person.

He shook himself. No point dwelling on that. He'd been good at pushing all thoughts of heartbreak from his mind for years and had other worries right now anyway. Not job worries, thankfully. He managed the surf shop his parents had bought over twenty years ago and he liked working there. It helped that he enjoyed surfing and the shop was close to the beach, so as soon as he finished work, he could grab his surfboard and head down to the water. He also had friends who'd stayed in Sea Breeze Sands and so life had remained mostly unchanged since he was a teenager when he'd worked in the shop part time, fitting it around school and then college. Some people would hate to live the way he did, working where he'd always worked, still living near his parents – he had the flat above the shop – and still seeing the same villagers every day. But Theo liked the familiarity of his routine and being near the people he loved and cared about. He'd never had ambitions to leave the beautiful location, unlike some people, and he doubted he ever would. Of course, his lack of ambition had come with a price because it hadn't made his first love happy, but he'd known he couldn't change how he felt about his home because then he'd have been lying to himself. He could have compromised, yes, but he'd been young and stubborn, and they'd been through such a painful experience that home had been the thing he'd clung to, while for her, running away had been easier.

Sighing, he pushed his shoulders back and went to the door. He opened it and gazed out at the street. The wooden planters were bursting with colourful blooms and birds sang in the trees. The air was fresh and sweet with notes of brine from the sea. The urge to jog down to the beach tingled through him. Theo could always lose himself swimming in the water, when he caught and rode a wave, when he felt the sea surround him as he plunged beneath the surface and let his cares fade away.

His phone buzzed on the counter, so he crossed the

shopfloor, picked it up and checked the screen. It was his mum letting him know that his nan fancied some chicken soup for tea and asking him to pick up some fresh bread from the baker a few doors down.

His heart squeezed as he replied, sending love to his mum and nan. At eighty-four, his nan, Barbara, was very frail. She'd always been a strong and independent woman but since being diagnosed with pancreatic cancer, she'd changed dramatically. She'd had pain medication and treatment to slow the disease but that had taken its toll on her and now she was declining quickly, which was why Willow and Daniel had brought their wedding forwards. They wanted Barbara to be there for their special day and so wedding planning was going full steam ahead.

Even though he had his own flat, Theo went back to his parents' home every day after work and on his days off to sit with his nan while he read to her or they watched TV. Every day, without fail, she asked if he had a girlfriend and told him that he should follow his heart and be with the woman he'd always loved. Theo had stopped trying to protest because when it came to his love life, his nan didn't want to hear the truth. She wanted to know that her only grandson was happy and settled just like her granddaughter. Theo wished he could grant her this wish with all his heart, but how could he when the only woman she wanted to see him with was the one woman he couldn't imagine reaching out to after so long?

Some things were just too hard to do and, sadly, this was one of them.

Willow

'Have you heard from her yet?' Lottie Treharne peered at Willow over her reading glasses.

'Mum, I've only just got here. Can I at least take my jacket off first?'

Lottie gave a brief smile then led the way through to the kitchen. 'Sorry, darling, I just want to know if she's coming.'

In the kitchen, Willow shrugged out of her suit jacket and hung it on the back of one of the chairs at the table. Her parents lived in a large house that had been extended over the years to include a spacious kitchen-diner that led onto a sunroom with bifold doors opening out onto the pretty garden. Her parents had worked hard all their lives, her mum as an accountant and her dad as a police officer, as well as overseeing the running of the surf shop by several different managers before Theo took over. As well as working, they'd striven to turn the once dated property into a beautiful home, and now they were both retired, they had time to enjoy it. Although *enjoy* wasn't exactly something she saw them doing very much of right now. They always looked so worried and harried and she knew that her nan's declining health had a lot to do with that. Willow was heartbroken seeing the change in her nan, but for her mum, to see her own mother struggling must be incredibly difficult, and also for her dad – who had lost his own parents many years ago – she knew that Barbara had been like a mum to him.

And it was one of the reasons why Willow hoped that the wedding would bring some joy to their lives. Of course, it would be bittersweet because they'd brought it forwards so her nan could be there, but a wedding was something to focus on and to celebrate and even though she was sad that her nan was so frail, she was also excited about marrying the man she loved.

Willow pulled the chair out and sat down then laced her fingers on the table in front of her. 'Right... in answer to your question... I received a reply late last night and yes... Chloe has agreed to come and to be a bridesmaid.'

Her mum filled the kettle then turned to her and nodded. 'That's good. I'm happy for your, darling, and happy for Mum. She so wants to see her.'

'I know. I felt a bit strange asking Chloe to come and to be a bridesmaid... I mean, we used to be so close but I haven't spoken to her properly in ages. We've commented on each other's Facebook posts from time to time but not had an actual conversation. Not that she posts much because she seems to be a really private person, but she did congratulate me on getting engaged.'

'You were the best of friends as children and long into your teens.'

'I know.' Willow swallowed hard, feeling the old sadness raising its head again. 'I loved her like a sister.'

'She spent a lot of time here... especially when she and Theo... got together.'

'Does he know I've invited her?'

'We have spoken about it, but you know Theo... he can be such a closed book so I'm not sure how he feels. Yet another reason why I worry so much about him.'

'Me too.' Willow thought about her older brother, the man who'd once been her tormentor, teasing her mercilessly when they were younger then who'd grown into her protector, constantly seeking to ensure that she was safe and well. Theo had insisted on picking her up from parties when she was a teenager and making sure she got home safe, telling his friends to back off and leave her alone when they noticed that she was no longer their friend's little sister but a young woman. And while that had been happening, Chloe had been growing up too, and one day, Theo seemed to notice that Chloe was a woman grown and had asked her out on a date. At first, Willow had found her brother and her best friend dating strange, but then, as Chloe and Theo had grown closer and nothing had really changed – because Chloe had been at their home so often anyway – it had felt like the natural direction for things to take.

'I'll tell him that she's accepted and see if he'll talk to me about it. I know it won't be easy for him being in the same place as her, but it's been, what... eleven or twelve years since they broke up?'

'About that. But it was all very... complicated.' Her mum placed two mugs of tea on the table then sat opposite Willow. 'There was more to it than we realised at the time.'

'Poor Theo. And poor Chloe. She lost us all when they split, didn't she?'

Her mum chewed at her bottom lip. 'I did contact her and tell her we were there for her, but I think she just felt too awkward to stay in touch.'

Willow sipped her tea, wincing as it burnt her tongue. 'Do you think the reason Theo hasn't settled down with anyone is because he still has feelings for Chloe?' It was something she'd wondered many times over the years and suspected to be true.

'It could be. I've spoken to your dad about it more than once, but we agreed that we're not sure that Theo even understands it all himself. It might be easier if we knew how Chloe felt about it but we can hardly bring it up with her after all this time, can we?'

'I don't think so...' Willow's stomach fluttered. She was actually a bit anxious about seeing Chloe again, and yet she was also looking forward to being reunited with her. Growing up, they'd shared so much and she'd grieved the loss of her friend in her life even though she'd also been hurt by how Chloe had walked away from their friendship when she'd split with Theo. But if there was ever a time when they were going to try to repair things between them, then surely it would be at Willow's wedding? 'Anyway... how's Nan today?'

Her mum rubbed her hands over her face and Willow saw the strain of recent months in her mum's eyes and her skin. She'd always looked younger than her years but now the skin around her eyes was crepey and dark, the lines around her mouth deeper, her collar bones more pronounced from her weight loss.

'She's resting at the moment.' Her mum gestured at the doorway that led off the kitchen to the smaller of the reception rooms. They'd turned it into a bedroom for her nan so she wouldn't have to climb the stairs and could easily access the downstairs wet room that led off the kitchen diner. 'But she's been tired today. Even more than usual.'

Willow reached across the table and took her mum's hand. 'I love you.'

'I love you too, sweetheart.'

'Are you sure the wedding isn't too much on top of what you're dealing with?'

Her mum smiled. 'Willow... your wedding is what's keeping me and your dad going right now. With Nan being so poorly, the wedding is the rainbow on the horizon, and I can't wait to be there when you and Daniel say your vows. To be honest... I also think it's what's keeping Nan hanging on.'

'Oh Mum...' Willow's throat tightened and her vision blurred.

'It'll all be OK in the end, Willow. We have to believe that. Nan has had a good life and a long life compared to some people, and seeing you married will be the icing on her cake.'

Willow covered her face with her hands. She was trying to be strong for her parents, trying to focus on her wedding planning and on getting everything just right, but sometimes things overwhelmed her. Her mum's bravery was inspirational but it made her feel like a little girl again, back when her mum seemed so strong and together, as if she could heal the world with one of her wonderful hugs.

And as if she knew what Willow was thinking, her mum was suddenly at her side, wrapping her arms around Willow and squeezing her tight. Willow hugged her right back as tears ran down her cheeks. Life could be painful, but if you had love then you had something to cling to, come what may.

Chloe

Driving towards Sea Breeze Sands, Chloe's gut churned as if she'd eaten a spicy curry. She hadn't been back in a while but not much had changed. The fields and hedgerows bordered familiar country lanes; the scents of flora and fauna and rich fertile earth that entered through the open windows were familiar; the sense of openness in the sky that spread out ahead seemingly endlessly, as she crested the hill then descended towards the village, was the same as it had always been. And yet... there was something different about it all. She'd avoided coming back for extended periods of time and when she had returned, she'd done so discretely to avoid drawing attention to her presence. So to return today, following her acceptance of Willow's invitation, which meant that people would know she was coming back, made her heart flutter and her palms clammy.

Chloe had told her mum and nan that she was taking an early finish for the summer to come back for the wedding and they'd both been delighted, especially when she'd told them that she was to be Willow's bridesmaid. She knew they'd both been saddened by how things had gone all those years ago and that they'd have liked to have her stay in the village, but they also knew that she wanted to leave, to live somewhere else, to try a different kind of life. They loved her and they understood that there was a whole world out there that Chloe wanted to experience. The irony of it was that although she had gone away with that aim in mind, she hadn't travelled extensively, had got distracted by work and the responsibilities that came with being an adult and ultimately, she had found that life wasn't that different in Reading than it had been in Cornwall. Of course, the surroundings were different – the vibrant city was very different to the rugged landscape of the north coast of Cornwall – but life itself was the same: she got up, got dressed, ate breakfast then went to work, except for at the weekends that were filled with washing, cleaning, reading and Netflix. She still got tired, hungry and hormonal, but she didn't have the comfort of her female relatives to wrap around herself like a warm hug, and instead had to fend for herself, to comfort herself and to manage alone. And that had been fine; she was strong and independent but there were days when the idea of her gran's homemade lasagne or her mum's gingerbread hot chocolate with marshmallows seemed to sing to her like a siren from afar, attempting to enchant her so she'd come home again. But there had always been the fear of crashing against the rocks of her past and so she'd stayed away as much as possible. There were certain things she knew she would always miss, and so she was glad that she'd have the opportunity to enjoy them while she was back in Sea Breeze Sands.

Chloe pulled into a layby to let a tractor heading in the opposite direction pass, and thought about her reply to Willow when she'd accepted the invite. It had taken courage to send that message to Willow, and she'd wondered for a moment if her old friend had only invited her to be kind. However, Willow's reply had been typically Willow, filled with exclamation marks and emojis and Chloe's heart had squeezed with nostalgia. She used to get Willow's messages all the time and it wasn't until this one that she realised how much she'd missed her old friend, how much receiving a text from her could lift her spirits and make her feel... happy. Even if just for a brief time because then she remembered why she was going home and what it might involve, and that filled her with trepidation.

Willow had asked to meet with her that Saturday so they could discuss wedding plans and dress fittings, and Chloe had been able to understand how much this meant to Willow. In that instant, she had vowed to do her best to be a wonderful brides-maid, made a promise to herself that she wouldn't let Willow down. It would be challenging for Chloe in a variety of ways, but she would ensure that Willow had no regrets about entrusting her with such an important role.

As teenagers, they'd often spoken about their dream men, about how one day they would marry for love and live happily ever after. But as Chloe had got older, she hadn't been convinced that settling down – especially if it involved living in the coastal village – was right for her. Her dreams had developed, she had wanted more and believed that life would be different away from the location where she'd grown up. Time had taught her that people were pretty much the same wherever they lived, and that life still came with the same stresses and demands. On occasion, she had actually wished she could go back to Sea Breeze Sands to live, to be near to her mum and gran, but then she'd tried to push that yearning away because what was the point in wishing for something that couldn't ever happen? How could she go back there when there were so many ghosts that would haunt her and when she would make others uncomfortable with her very presence?

And so she had tried to get on with her life in Reading, tried to appreciate what she had, until she'd received Willow's text and known that she couldn't pretend any longer. Sometimes in life, something happened that made it impossible to continue as you were, and in this case it had been Willow's message.

She changed gear as she drove down the steep hill then followed the curve of the road towards the village. In the after-noon light, the sun made the rooftops glow like they'd been painted with gold and the sea glistened invitingly. How long had it been since she'd kicked off her shoes and splashed in the shallows? Since she'd stripped off and run into the waves? How long since she'd lain on the sand, her hair and bikini wet, the taste of salt on her lips as the sun warmed her skin? Since she felt free?

Such simple pleasures were ones she missed when she allowed herself to consider them. Perhaps she could indulge those longings over the duration of her stay. She'd finished work weeks before the end of term, apologising to the supply teaching agency and claiming a family emergency that meant she had to go home. They'd been very understanding. Chloe was reliable and hardworking; schools had asked for her more than once and so the agency knew that she was good to have on their books. They'd said that they hoped to see her in September and would certainly have plenty of work for her. Chloe had thanked them but been unable to think that far ahead. Her focus was on the here and now and that was as far as it could go at the moment because the wedding was such a big event in her social calendar. In her life calendar.

She kept her eyes fixed ahead as she drove through the village, passing pubs and shops, houses belonging to people she'd known over the years, heading towards the end of the village where the properties were further apart and where she knew a warm welcome would be waiting. More than anything right now she just wanted a hug from her gran and one from her mum. Only then would she feel fortified and ready to prepare for seeing familiar faces again.

At least, that was the plan...

Theo

'Hello?' Theo called as he entered his parents' home.

'Hi love,' his mum replied as she appeared in the kitchen doorway. Her normally neat grey bob was tousled as if she'd dragged her hands through it and she was wearing her reading glasses perched on the end of her rather red nose.

'You OK?' Theo approached her cautiously, aware that her moods currently changed promptly depending upon how things were with his nan. One minute his mum could be laughing, the next she'd lock herself in the toilet with 'an upset stomach' that Theo knew translated as 'to have a good cry'.

She blinked, rubbed a hand over her face then sniffed hard. 'Yup. I'm fine. Just a bit... tired.'

'Bad night?'

She inclined her head a fraction, clearly not wanting to admit that she'd barely slept.

'Well I'm here now so why don't you go and have a nap or a bath? Relax for a bit.'

He saw her falter, glance in the direction of the lounge.

'Where's Nan?'

'Watching TV.'

'I'll sit with her. You go and do what you need to do.'

'I have a pile of ironing.' His mum held her hand up in front of her. 'A mountain actually. I need to get through it or it will keep building and then it will stress me out and—'

'Mum, you don't have to do that now.'

'I do, love. If I don't get it done it'll be worse tomorrow.' She sagged on the spot as if even staying upright was too difficult.

'Look... you go and rest and I'll do it while I watch TV with Nan.'

'Really?' His mum's eyes filled with tears as if the thought that she wouldn't need to tackle the ironing was an enormous relief.

'Absolutely. Let me get the ironing board set up in the lounge then you go and run a bath.' He opened his arms and pulled her into a hug.

'Thank you, Theo. You're such a good son.' She stepped back and wiped her eyes with the back of her hand.

He smiled. 'I just want to help.'

'The ironing is mainly bedding. I'm stripping Nan's bed quite often right now because I like her to have nice fresh sheets.'

'Why're you ironing bedding?'

'Can't stand the thought of anyone sleeping on wrinkled sheets.' She gave a small laugh. 'Especially not my mother. Am I mad?'

'Just a bit.' He winked to show he was teasing. 'Right... let me get organised.' He took his denim jacket off and hung it on the banister then went through to the lounge. 'Hello Nan!'

His nan peered up at him from the chair near the window. She looked so tiny that his breath caught in his throat. Even though he saw her every day, he still struggled to accept how changed she was, how each day seemed to drain her a little bit more. Her wrinkled face broke into a grin and his heart lurched.

'Theo.' She held up her arms and he went over to her and gave her a gentle hug. She felt like a tiny sparrow in his arms and her fluffy hair tickled her cheek as he turned to give her a kiss.

'What're you watching?' He sat back on his haunches and glanced at the TV.

'It's an old movie.'

'I can see that.' He frowned at the 50-inch flatscreen where a gritty black and white movie was flickering. 'Was it made when the Vikings invaded?'

His nan chuckled. 'Round about then.'

'You'd have been twenty-one, right?'

She tapped his arm. 'You cheeky so and so.'

'I'm teasing you, Nan.'

'I know, my darling. Are you here for dinner?' The hope in her voice tugged at his heartstrings.

'I'm here for the entire evening and completely at your disposal.'

'Goody.' She clapped her hands then sat back on the chair as if the simple action had exhausted her.

'I've offered to help mum with the ironing so I'll go and grab what I need and be straight back. Can I get you a cup of tea or something?'

She turned her brown eyes to him. 'Ummm... A cup of that mint tea would be nice. It seems to help settle my stomach.' She placed a hand on her abdomen and winced as if even the softest touch could cause pain.

'Mint tea coming right up.'

Theo left the room quickly, hoping that his nan hadn't seen the tears in his eyes or the way he knew his face had fallen when he saw her pain. In the hallway, he leant against the wall while he took some slow, deep breaths. It was so difficult seeing his nan suffering and he'd have taken her pain in a second if he could have done. They'd lost his grandpa to a heart attack ten years ago and it had been dreadful, but then so was this. His nan had been diagnosed just months ago but it felt like years. She'd been suffering from stomach pain for a while but had failed to tell anyone about it until it was so bad she passed out while putting the washing on the line in her garden. Luckily, his mum had been there and she'd called for an ambulance immediately. Hospital checks had led to the cancer diagnosis and treatment options. The word options seemed ironic in light of the fact that none of them provided the option they all wanted – to see his nan recover and live for another decade or more. However, after an initial treatment that made her feel worse, his nan had declined any further treatment apart from pain relief. The consultant had told her that surgery was unlikely to help because the cancer was advanced, and while she could try chemo to slow the cancer and improve the symptoms, it wouldn't cure it. After listening to the information, Barbara had asked her daughter and son-in-law to take her home where she'd made a cup of tea and sat quietly. Finally, she'd told them that she didn't want chemo, that she'd lived a good life and that this was nature's way of telling her that her time was up. She wanted to die with dignity not prolong the suffering for her and her loved ones.

Initially, Theo's family had protested and tried to persuade her to change her mind but Barbara could be stubborn and her mind was made up, so they all coped in different ways. His mum had rushed around trying to make everything perfect for her family, wearing herself out every day so she fell into bed exhausted every night. His dad had done his best to take care of things like getting one of the ground floor rooms ready for his mother-in-law so she could stay with them, sorting her house and finances, preparing everything so she didn't have to worry. Theo had kept the surf shop running and helped his parents out with things like food shopping and filling the cars with fuel, mowing the grass and visiting daily. And Willow had brought her wedding forwards in the hope that their nan would be able to attend, something Theo knew his nan was delighted about.

He rubbed his fists over his eyes and sighed. Life could be wonderful and it could be hard and this was one of the hardest things he'd been through. Losing Chloe had been tough and he'd grieved for her and their relationship; losing his grandpa had been very sad and sudden, and somehow, he had coped, but this was tough. His nan was fading, leaving them slowly and it made Theo wonder what was worse – to go suddenly or to die slowly, knowing it was coming and that your time was limited. Of course, no one knew how long they had left but his nan knew for certain that she didn't have long to go.

A tear trickled down his cheek and he wiped it away, stood up straight and rolled his shoulders. There would be time for crying and grieving in the future but for now his nan was here, waiting for him in the lounge, and he wanted to join her as soon as possible. He headed for the kitchen to make tea and grab the ironing board and iron, making a conscious effort to push his sadness away. He would be Theo the joker, the loving grandson, the man he knew his family needed him to be right now. His own grieving would have to wait.

Chloe

~∾∾⌒

Chloe parked her car and sat quietly for a moment, gazing out towards the sea. Her gran's home was in an elevated position with a panoramic view of the coastal path, cliffs and the sea beyond. Behind her cottage was the village of Sea Breeze Sands. It was a beautiful location and Chloe had enjoyed growing up there, sitting in the window seat and gazing out at the sea through the seasons, as well as being just a short walk from the beach. She'd dreamt about Sea Breeze Sands often over the years, as if while she consciously tried to put it from her mind, her heart and subconscious couldn't let go of their longing for the place – for the people who lived there.

Adjoining her gran's cottage was the gift shop that her gran had opened many years ago, way before Chloe was born. It had grown from being a shop that sold a few random knick-knacks to one that sold desirable local wares like pottery, sea glass jewellery, paintings (some by Chloe's mum) and a variety of clothing items and accessories. Chloe never knew what she'd find in there when she came home, and one time, she'd even found her gran selling homegrown potatoes and carrots as she had an abundance in her garden. Well, her gran claimed to be selling them, but Chloe knew that Nora Nancarrow was actually giving them away to anyone who needed them. Her gran had run a form of foodbank long before such things had been widespread, and had always done whatever she could to assist those who'd fallen on hard times. And people did struggle, even in a pretty village like this. Those who relied on tourism had to accept that some months of the year would be busier than others; fishing could be an unreliable income for some with ups and downs throughout the year; others had lost their jobs due to ill health and then there were locals who needed a helping hand because they were simply getting older. Chloe's gran had recently turned seventy-five but she'd always been fit and strong, a yoga enthusiast since the sixties, and with her lithe frame, glowing skin and sparkly eyes she didn't look much older than Chloe's mum, Stella Redgrave. In fact, the two could have been sisters with just a few years between them. Her mum had told her on many occasions that Nora had been mistaken for being her older sister and it had grated on her nerves as a teenager, but as she'd got older, she'd enjoyed it.

Chloe got out of the car and stretched her legs. Even with frequent stops at service stations, the journey had still been arduous and with the stops it had taken her over five hours. But she was here now and there would be plenty of time to rest and relax, to walk and to enjoy the sea air.

She grabbed her suitcase from the boot, locked the car then headed towards the cottage. Her gran would probably have closed the shop for the day, so she'd just as well go straight to the cottage. As she walked, her stomach grumbled and she smiled, thinking of her gran's home cooking and of the hugs that awaited her inside.

At the front door, she knocked gently then pushed the handle and went in. She had her own key but the door was rarely locked during the day so she hadn't even bothered to get it out of her bag.

'Hello? Mum? Gran? I'm here.'

She placed her suitcase against the wall near the bottom of the stairs and removed her purple hoodie. The hallway hadn't changed at all and still smelt of cinnamon and beeswax polish, of baking and coffee. It was a heady combination that shouted *home* as it wrapped itself around her and she closed her eyes and breathed it in.

'What're you doing standing there with your eyes closed?'

She grinned as she opened her eyes to find her gran standing in front of her with a tea towel in her hands.

'Gran!' She hugged her gran tight, inhaling the familiar rose water perfume as the older woman hugged her back.

'Let me look at you, Chloe.' Her gran leant back and appraised her, pushed her hair behind her ears and turned her face from side to side. 'You look a bit skinny. Haven't you been eating?'

'Of course, I have. You know me... appetite of a horse.'

'Hmmmm.' Her gran's grey eyes met Chloe's and a small line appeared between her brows. 'A few of my double chocolate chip brownies will put some colour into your cheeks.'

'Yum!'

'Come on through to the kitchen and have a mug of Earl Grey and a brownie and you can tell me all about your journey.'

Chloe let her gran lead her by the hand as if she was a child again, enjoying the feeling of being looked after. She'd been raised by her mum and her gran after her dad had died in a fishing accident when she was twelve. Overwhelmed by grief, and struggling financially, her mum had moved back in with Nora and never left. It had suited the three of them because they had the comfort of family around them that they all craved and Chloe loved being around her gran, helping her in the shop and baking with her at weekends. Her gran was a fascinating woman with plenty of stories – some that Chloe believed were real and some that were clearly made up, like the ones about the fairies that had their bower along the coastal path and the dragon that lived in a cave that could be accessed from the beach when the tide was out. Nora had always warned Chloe never to go to the cave alone in case she encountered the dragon. As Chloe had got older, she'd realised it was because when the tide came in, the cave was completely cut off from the mainland and filled with water that meant anyone in there would have to tread water for hours to survive or swim out towards the beach. This in itself was dangerous because of the strong tides and waves that could sweep even the strongest swimmer out to sea. It had happened several times over the years and a teenaged boy, drunk on cider had been carried to his death; a man trying to rescue his dog had been swept out but thankfully rescued by the lifeboat crew – they'd saved his dog too. There was also a rumour that a woman had thrown herself from the cliffs back in the 1800s as she tried to escape her domineering husband. It was a tragic tale and one that Chloe had always thought to be very sad and one she hoped wasn't true. As with all small seaside villages, there were myths and legends as well as anecdotes aplenty, some happy and some sad, but Chloe had learnt that life was like that and appreciating the good times was the best way to keep going.

'Right, sit yourself down and I'll make tea.'

Her gran gestured at the window seat with its plump red cushions and red and white checked curtains and Chloe did so gratefully, leaning her back against the thick whitewashed wall.

The kitchen was cosy with a low ceiling and exposed beams, old oak cupboards, the AGA against the chimney breast, the apron fronted sink in front of the window overlooking the gravel patch where people parked their cars when visiting the shop. The round table with four chairs had been against the internal wall for as long as Chloe could remember and she knew that if she looked at its surface, it would read like a family history with its grooves and marks from years of letters, accounts, designs and homework that had been completed on its surface. Chloe had run her fingertips over the worn surface many times, feeling the indentations of family life engraved upon it. There was something incredibly comforting about the table and its scars. Her gran had refused to get a new one when Chloe's mum had suggested it, stating that she loved the stories the table had to tell. Some people seemed to be obsessed with buying new things all the time, as if such things could fill a void that existed inside them, but Nora was a firm believer in if it's not broken then why fix it? It was also why Nora had rarely decorated the cottage, again referring to how some people decorated every year as if that too could make them complete or allow them to forget about their troubles. Nora's solution for worries was a long walk in the fresh air, a mug of tea, a hug and a good book. It had always worked for Chloe, at least most of the time, although some things simply had to be endured until the pain faded and life got back to some sort of normal again.

'Here you go, my darling.' Nora handed Chloe a mug of tea and a small china plate with an enormous chocolate brownie on it.

'That brownie will put at least half a stone on me.' Chloe eyed it, thinking about the calories it contained even as her mouth watered.

'And? You need it, Chloe, believe me.'

Her gran got her own tea and brownie then joined Chloe on the window seat. They faced each other, both tucking their legs underneath them as they'd always done. Chloe took a bite of brownie. The rich dark chocolate and fudgy texture were perfect and she moaned with pleasure. 'This is gorgeous.'

'Glad you like it. It's a vegan recipe I've been experimenting with.'

'Vegan?'

Her gran nodded. 'Got to do what we can to help the planet. We've been drinking plant-based milk now for months and I can't tell the difference. Try your tea.'

Chloe took a sip and frowned. 'Tastes fine.'

'It's oat milk. Good, isn't it?'

'Lovely. You could sell the brownies.'

'Your mum and I have been talking about that and about the possibility of setting up a mail order brownie service. Something to consider anyway. I'd need to get council approval and to have someone to help out in the shop so I could bake but it's just an idea for us to consider.'

'Sounds like a good one.' Chloe put her brownie down and licked her fingers. 'I've just realised I didn't ask where Mum is. I was so happy to be home that I completely forgot.'

Her gran's eyes drifted towards the window and Chloe followed her gaze. With its view of the coastal path, cliffs and the sea, it had been Chloe's favourite reading spot growing up. She'd loved curling up there under a throw with a good book, a mug of tea or hot chocolate, and reading for hours. The lounge of the cottage had floor to ceiling bookshelves around every wall and the TV had rarely been on, except for when they watched movies at weekends.

'Gran?' Chloe leant towards Nora. 'Is Mum OK?'

'Oh... yes, Chloe.' Her gran met her eyes again and smiled but the smile seemed to falter. 'Your mum is out with a friend. She did say she'd be here for when you arrived but then we weren't sure exactly what time that would be. I'm sure she won't be long.'

'That's fine. I wasn't sure what time I'd get here, so that's understandable. Be nice to see her though.' Chloe thought of her mum with her long blonde hair and bright blue eyes, of how she always smelt like fresh air and honey. Nora lived in faded Levis, men's shirts and Crocs and kept her white hair short. On contrast, Stella wore her hair long and kept her roots touched up with a rich golden blonde. She wore flowing skirts with sequins and silver thread sewn into them, sheer silk tops over camisoles and colourful Doctor Marten boots that she'd decorated herself with elaborate patterns. She was what Nora described as bohemian, a free spirit that could never be tied down, which was why Nora had told Chloe many times that she'd been surprised when her daughter came home and told her she was getting married to Chloe's dad. Stella had been just eighteen, fresh out of college after studying Art and Design, and she'd abandoned her plans to go study art at university to stay in Sea Breeze Sands and be a mum. It had, Stella had told Chloe, been a decision she'd never regretted but she'd also been left destitute and heartbroken when her husband had died. She'd worked through her grief by moving back in with her mum, taking care of Chloe and painting dramatic landscapes that she sold in the shop, and for most of the time, she'd seemed happy. *Most of the time...* Chloe could remember the days when her mum had been sad, seeming distant and removed as if her mind was somewhere else. Chloe had known that at those times she needed to give her mum some space and so she'd seek out her gran and they'd do things together like comb the beach for sea glass or bake cakes they'd always wanted to try.

'She's looking forward to seeing you very much too.' Her gran smiled then munched on what was left of her brownie. 'Eat up then we can go for a walk because I'm sure you're desperate to get some good sea air into your lungs.'

'Sounds wonderful.' Chloe finished her brownie and drank her tea, pushing away the questions that had popped into her mind about her mum, like why had her gran seemed shifty when Chloe had asked about her, and was the friend she'd gone out with a bit more than just a friend?

Taking their plates and mug to the sink, she swilled them then dried her hands. 'I'll go and get my trainers on.'

'Grab a jacket too, Chloe, it'll be breezy down by the sea.'

'Will do.'

Chloe bobbed her head then left the kitchen and carried her suitcase upstairs to her old room. She grabbed her trainers that were right at the top of the case but left her unpacking until later, keen to head down to the beach and make the most of being home.

Theo

'I haven't a clue what I'm going to wear to the wedding.'

Theo looked over at his nan. 'I'm sure Mum will help you find something.'

'From my wardrobe, I hope, because there's no point splashing out on an outfit now.'

'Of course there is, Nan. Now, more than ever, you should get glammed up.'

His nan ran a hand over her fluffy hair. 'Wonder if they can do anything with this. It's like candyfloss. I don't want to look a dreadful mess on the wedding photos. Imagine Willow's children looking back on them in years to come and asking who the scary old woman is.' She chuckled and Theo shook his head but he couldn't help smiling. It was bittersweet that his nan would be at the wedding because while it would be wonderful to have her there, the fact that she was so ill was incredibly sad.

Theo picked another pillowcase from the basket and ran the iron over it. Steam floated into the air like a fragranced cloud then disappeared as if it had never been there.

'It's still light,' his nan said, looking out of the window. 'I do love the summer evenings. Winter always gets me down when it's dark by four or earlier, as well as dark when you wake up in the morning.'

'Winter's never easy.' Theo sighed, thinking of how it limited his time in the water and always reminded him of the things he missed from his past. Like Chloe and what they'd had. The dreams he'd treasured of their future together. The security he'd felt in their relationship and how much better the nights had seemed when he'd been able to hold her close.

'How much ironing do you have left?'

Theo peered into the basket on the floor next to the ironing board.

'Two pillowcases it looks like.' He looked at the sofa where the ironing he'd done sat in neat piles.

'You got through that quickly.' His nan grinned. 'You'll make someone a fine husband.'

'Hmmm.' He raised his eyebrows then picked another pillowcase from the basket and set it on the ironing board.

'I wish I could go for a walk,' his nan said, tilting her head as she gazed at him.

'A walk?' His voice went up at the end, his surprise evident.

'Yes. It's been weeks since I've been anywhere other than medical appointments and I'd love to get some fresh air.'

Theo thought quickly. Was she *able* to go for a walk? She was very weak and she tired easily. He'd tried to tempt her out for a while but she often made excuses and so he'd stopped trying, not wanting to put pressure on her. There was the wheelchair, though...

'Where do you fancy going?' he asked, folding the pillowcase and placing it on the pile.

'To the beach.' The twinkle in her eyes told him that she was serious, and he could understand how she felt. Being cooped up inside all the time wasn't good for anyone and so he'd do what he could to help her.

'Let me put all this away then we'll get you wrapped up warm and take the wheelchair down to the seafront. I can drive us there then push you down to the sand.'

'Are you sure you don't mind? I don't want to be any trouble.'

'Nan...' He smiled. 'You could never be any trouble. I love you and I want to make you happy. I'd do anything for you.'

'I know that, love, I know,' she said. 'But first, could you get my bag for me?'

'Your bag?'

'It's in my room.'

'Oh... OK...'

'I want to put some makeup on. I can't go out looking like this because people will talk.'

'People will talk?' Theo swallowed a chuckle. What did people matter?

'A lady has to look her best, Theo.' She winked at him and he winked back.

He left the lounge and walked through the kitchen to his nan's room, a grin on his face because it was good that she wanted to go out and good that she wanted to look her best. It was the strength and pride that she'd shown all his life and although it had waned a bit recently as her illness had drained her, it seemed that nothing – not even cancer – could steal the courage or spirit of the amazing little woman he was proud to call Nan.

Chloe

'I often think I remember how beautiful it is here then when I come home, I'm always stunned by exactly how beautiful it is,' Chloe said, as she stood with her hands on the rail of the path overlooking the beach. Steps led from the path to the sand at one end of the beach, in the middle was a concrete ramp used to get boats and sometimes vehicles down to the beach, and at the other end were sand dunes.

'Nothing like a Sea Breeze Sands evening.' Her gran rested her arms on the rail next to Chloe and they gazed out at the horizon. The sky was painted with shades of apricot and pink and daubed with burnt orange strokes.

'I'm sure I've seen a painting of Mum's that looks just like this.'

'Oh you know your mum; she's painted a thousand Sea Breeze Sands landscapes and every single one takes my breath away.'

'With her talent it's a shame she never did more with her art.'

Her gran sighed then turned to face Chloe. 'I agree in some ways, but I also think that she did the right thing at the time for her, and for you. If she hadn't fallen in love with your dad then she wouldn't have had you, and if she hadn't had you then... our lives would be far duller. You were meant to be conceived and I'm so glad you were.'

Chloe smiled. 'Me too.'

'I know things have been difficult for your mum over the years and that when she lost your dad, she was bereft, but they did love each other deeply. She loved and she lost, but wasn't it better that she did love him that much than never knowing that feeling? I certainly think so. Sometimes, I wish I'd known love like that. And then I think I'm glad I didn't because losing someone when you love them that deeply is dreadful. And now I'm contradicting myself.' She laughed and Chloe joined in.

'Are you saying that it's OK for Mum to love and grieve but not for you?'

Her gran cocked an eyebrow. 'That's what it sounded like, I know. What I meant was that your mum and dad were meant to be together. They adored each other and I can't imagine them not being together. However... for me... it was different. As you know, your grandfather was a summer fling that never amounted to anything. He was handsome, sophisticated, mysterious and older than me and I enjoyed being with him for a short time but I never imagined myself in love with him. I was terrified when I found myself pregnant but there was no way I'd have considered trying to do anything about it, and your mum became the centre of my world when she was born. I could have had relationships... I had several offers over the years, but I just didn't want to know.'

Chloe watched her gran's face, her skin warm with the glow of the sun, her eyes seeming lit from within by the apricot and orange. 'You didn't need a man to feel complete,' she said, understanding.

'That's right. I always felt comfortable enough in my own skin not to need someone else and I tried to instil that same confidence in your mum and in you.'

'I never felt that I *needed* a man...' Chloe let her sentence trail off.

'No, but when you fell in love with Theo, you fell hard.'

Chloe closed her eyes, trying to force the tears back into her tear ducts. She wouldn't cry now; she absolutely wouldn't. Being back here always brought buried emotions rushing back to the surface and it was a struggle to contain them. The familiar scenery, the joy of seeing her family, the air, the buildings, the sunsets... it all dug deep inside her and left her stomach churning, her heart fluttering, her throat tight. Theo and what they'd shared had been wonderful and then it hadn't been, and then there'd been... other reasons to walk away and keep going. Reasons she hadn't wanted to keep thinking about and had hoped a change of scenery, a different lifestyle would keep from her mind. But sooner or later, it seemed, such reasons would find their way into her conscious mind and make her feel their impact all over again.

'It's OK to still have feelings about him and... well, you know?'

Chloe opened her eyes and met her gran's wise gaze.

'I know. It's just that coming home stirs things up for me. Not that I still have... well... I don't love Theo anymore, obviously. I can't possibly still love him after so much time, can I?'

'Are you asking me or telling me?' Her gran raised her eyebrows.

'Telling... I think. Or asking. Oh... I don't know.' Chloe rubbed her hands over her face and exhaled loudly. 'Ignore me, Gran, I'm just tired after the drive. I know I don't love Theo now. I just have my rose-tinted spectacles on and am feeling nostalgic.'

'So... you say you don't still love him, and I believe you believe that. But there might still be residual feelings there. After all, you did go through a lot together at important times in your lives. You were also the best of friends, so when you separated, you lost your partner *and* your best friend. It was a double loss.'

Chloe nodded, grateful that her gran had been able to articulate what she was struggling to put into words.

'Or even a triple loss.' The words hung in the air for a moment and Chloe wished she could put out a hand and wave them away, but her gran thankfully moved the conversation forwards. 'How do you feel about the wedding?'

'I'm really happy for Willow and Daniel.'

'I didn't mean that, but yes, it is lovely news. I meant—'

'I know what you meant, Gran, I was just stalling. I'm going to see Theo, be near Theo, have a whole load of feelings raked up. He might be there with someone and that will be... strange. But I'll deal with it because I'm a grownup and that's what grownups do.'

Her gran didn't reply but Chloe felt as if she could see right down into her heart. Nora had always been able to make Chloe feel as if her heart was exposed and as if she could read the truth in every word or attempt at misdirection that left Chloe's lips.

'I want to be there for Willow and it will be good to see her family again.' Chloe thought of Lottie and Mike Treharne, of how they'd been like family to her and how much she'd missed them when she'd left Theo and Sea Breeze Sands behind. And she thought of Barbara Rees, about how she'd adored Theo's nan and how the fact that she was so poorly was utterly devastating. The idea that the once strong and fiercely independent woman was unwell was painful for Chloe and as she gazed out at the sea, at the push and pull of the tide against the shore, she realised that it hadn't fully sunk in how abhorrent the idea of Barbara dying was. Everyone died, of course they did, but not people like Barbara – people who were so together, so determined and so precious. Losing Barbara was as terrible as the thought of losing her mum or her gran. It brought everything home to her and tugged at her heart until she worried it would fracture into a thousand pieces.

'Barbara isn't well, Chloe. You know that don't you?'

'Willow told me that's why they brought the wedding forwards.'

'You'll find her very changed. I've seen her a few times recently and even I was shocked and you know I don't shock easily.'

'I know.' Chloe sagged against the rail and gripped it for support. When her gran touched her shoulder, she turned and buried herself in her gran's embrace.

'I just wanted to make sure you were ready for seeing her, that's all.' Her gran patted her back gently as she'd done when she was a child. 'And I'll be there with you at the wedding, as will your mum. We've all been invited.'

'Yes.' Chloe held on tight to her gran, wanting to be reassured that nothing would ever separate them, that her gran wasn't getting older and wouldn't get ill, yearning for the innocence of childhood again. If only she could go back to the time before her dad passed away, back when she'd believed that her parents and gran were immortal and would always be around. Losing her dad had shaken that faith but she'd grown to live with her loss, adapted to be resilient, and the things that had happened over the years had built on that inner strength and resilience. Being wrapped up in the love of her mum and gran, two strong and caring women, had helped with that. But now and then, like right now, she felt it all over again like a giant wave that swept her off her feet, sucked her under and stole her breath away.

Life was often difficult but a hug from a loved one helped. The next few weeks would bring their own challenges but with her mum and her gran at her side, Chloe would square her shoulders, lift her chin and face whatever came her way. It was how her mum and her gran had taught her to live, and even when she had wobbles, she'd still keep on keeping on.

Theo

It took Theo a while to get his nan down to the sea front but they made it eventually, just as the sun was setting. He parked in the car park that overlooked the beach then cut the engine. Next to him in the passenger seat, his nan clapped her hands together.

'Oh look, Theo... how glorious.'

The sun was low, seeming to rest just above the surface of the water and the deep orange glow spread over the surface of the sea so it was hard to tell where the sky ended and the sea began. The edges of the orange blended with shades of lavender and peacock blue, creating a perfect palette of colours.

'It's wonderful, isn't it?'

'Thank you for bringing me down here.'

'We'll have to do it more often. Every day you feel up to it, in fact.'

His nan turned to him then raised her hand and cupped his cheek, but she didn't reply. She didn't need to.

'I'll get the chair out then we can go down to the sand.'

'OK.'

When he'd set the chair next to the passenger door, Theo reached into the back of the car for his rucksack and the warm blanket he'd brought. Even though the evening was mild, he knew his nan would feel the cold so had come prepared. He hung the rucksack on the back of the chair and tucked the blanket under his arm.

As he straightened up, movement at the far end of the beach caught his eye and he squinted against the evening brightness, suddenly aware that the two figures looked familiar.

Was that...

Could it be Chloe?

The world seemed to rock beneath his trainers and he sucked in a shaky breath. He knew Chloe would be coming back for the wedding because Willow had told him, but actually seeing her was very different to imagining how it would feel. He'd seen her a few times over the years but done his best to avoid bumping into her and assumed she'd done the same with him. She never came into the surf shop and he never went to her gran's shop. He'd seen her gran and her mum out and about and they were all very polite and courteous, which had seemed strange at first but then he'd grown used to it over the years so it had become almost normal. *Almost* because he'd loved Chloe so deeply that seeing her or her family and not being able to speak to them in the way he'd once done, not being able to hold Chloe close and kiss her soft lips, knowing that she'd never care for him as she once had was hard. When you'd once been close to another human being who then walked away from you and what you'd shared, it was difficult to overcome. Incredibly difficult and there were times when Theo wondered if he'd ever fully recovered. If he ever would.

He watched as Chloe and Nora climbed the steps that led to the coastal path, the ache in his heart growing with every second, then he dragged his gaze away from them and opened the car door. Now was not the time to long for the woman who'd broken his heart; there would be plenty of time for that over coming weeks when he'd be much closer to her than he was right now. When they would, in fact, be in the same room once more.

'Let me help you out, Nan.' He took her hands and helped

her into the chair then spread the blanket over her legs and tucked it around her. She'd worn a warm fleecy jacket, a bobble hat and gloves, so with the blanket he was confident that she'd be warm enough.

He locked up the car then pushed the chair towards the ramp that led down to the sand. The ramp was used to get boats down to the water and sometimes vehicles during the summer months when the village held events there. He took care not to slip on the worn, bumpy concrete. The idea of falling and losing his grip on the wheelchair and watching his nan careen down towards the sand, the bobble on her hat bouncing with the movement, then the impact when it hit the sand throwing her from the chair, made his heart lurch. He tightened his grip around the handles.

At the bottom of the ramp, Theo pushed the chair onto the sand but it dragged as he tried to move it forwards. He almost let out a grunt of frustration but swallowed it quickly, not wanting to upset his nan. He could try giving it a shove but again the image of his gran being catapulted forwards out of her chair made him shudder so he didn't want to risk it.

'Oh dear,' she said, 'Looks like we're stuck.'

Theo looked at the water, at the quiet expanse of beach, then at the chair. There was a plastic backed picnic blanket in the rucksack he'd brought along with a flask of tea and some biscuits. There was no way he was going to let the damp sand defeat him.

'No we're not,' he said, as he fastened the rucksack on his back. 'Get ready...'

'For what?' She knitted her brows. 'It's lovely right here, Theo. I'm so happy to be out again.'

He shook his head. 'I'm taking you down to the water's edge to drink your tea.'

'What?'

He slid his hands under her legs and scooped her up. A lump rose in his throat at how light she was, like a coat filled with feathers rather than a grown woman. She'd lost so much weight recently and it hit him exactly how poorly she was.

'Theo!' She chuckled as she wrapped her thin arms around his neck. 'Whatever are you doing?'

'Taking you to have tea and biscuits while we watch the sun set.'

He carried her to an appropriate spot then set her down gently, got the picnic blanket out of the rucksack and spread it out then helped his nan to sit down. He got the flask and biscuits out of the rucksack then set it behind his nan to support her back while he tucked the blanket around her again.

'How's that?' he asked, once he'd poured tea and handed her a cup.

'Absolutely perfect,' she replied, smiling at him. 'You're such a good grandson, Theo.'

He wrapped one arm around her then gazed at the horizon, trying hard to swallow against the emotion currently choking him. Simple things could make people happy and although he'd been shaken to see Chloe – even from a distance – he intended on making the most of this moment with his nan, enjoying her company and the beautiful sunset, being present and putting everything else from his mind.

For now, all that mattered was being here with this wonderful little woman.

Willow

Walking towards the beach café, Willow admired the colourful flowers filling the beds either side of the path. Their fragrance was sweet and uplifting and the June morning air was like a warm caress against her exposed skin. She'd put on a yellow summer dress, white plimsols and a white cardigan and wondered if she might need to remove the cardigan when she went inside.

The beach café was located in its own grounds a short walk from the beach. Even though it didn't overlook the beach, it was so named because of its proximity and because when the breeze blew in the right direction, you could smell the brine of the sea and sometimes even hear the waves as they crashed against the shore. The café was surrounded by well-established trees that provided privacy and shelter, and Willow had always found it a very relaxing place to visit.

As she reached the steps that led to the café door, she paused when her stomach gave a little flip. She'd come here to meet Chloe and hadn't thought she was feeling nervous, but now, the thought of seeing her old friend after so long suddenly seemed daunting. Would they still get on? Would Chloe be very changed? Would things be awkward between them, especially when it came to mentioning Theo?

Willow had, after all, asked Chloe to be her bridesmaid and that was a bold move after so much time had passed. Chloe could be completely different now after her time away from the village and that would make things strange for Willow and for her family. Not that having Chloe as her bridesmaid would be without some strangeness, but Willow had hoped it was the right thing to do.

She sucked in a deep breath then pushed open the door. There was only one way to find out if this would work.

Aromas of coffee and cake met her nostrils and her mouth watered. The comforting smells helped her to relax a bit and she looked around the café, searching for Chloe. She didn't appear to be there yet but then Willow was ten minutes early, so she took a seat at a corner table.

She'd walked to the café because it only took ten minutes from her house which was situated on the clifftop development. It was a beautiful new house that she and Daniel had bought just over a year ago and she loved living there. Prior to that, they'd rented a small cottage in the village while they'd saved and then waited for the Sea View site to be built. Willow knew she was lucky to have such a wonderful home but she had also worked hard to save the deposit, and so had Daniel, and she hoped that in time, they'd be able to share it with their children. Not immediately, because Willow still had a few things she wanted to achieve before she had children but she was thirty-two now and she felt that her clock was starting to tick a bit louder. Hopefully, she still had time and would be able to have children. She had friends and colleagues of the same age who either had two or three children already or who were finding it difficult to conceive and so she knew that parenthood didn't come easily for everyone. She kept herself fit and healthy, but she knew that despite this they could struggle to conceive. One of her colleagues had recently lost twins at eleven weeks pregnant and Willow's heart had broken for the woman and her partner as she'd known how excited they were about the thought of becoming parents. She'd witnessed the pain someone felt when they miscarried before, and it wasn't something she had believed she could deal with; it wasn't something she wanted to put Daniel through. And yet... to have a child they would need to face that risk so at some point, she'd have to brave it. But first, she had a wedding to plan in a short space of time and sorting out her one and only bridesmaid was a good step towards achieving that goal.

She pulled her phone from her bag and checked it in case Chloe had messaged but there was nothing other than a text from the bank offering her a credit card. She deleted it then put her phone away again and picked up a menu.

When the door opened, she looked up and smiled even as nerves made her armpits tingle.

There she was. Her old friend.

'Chloe!' she raised her hand and Chloe smiled in response then crossed the café to the table.

'Hello you.' Chloe's cheeks were pink and Willow wasn't sure if it was from the warmth or nerves. 'Gosh it's good to see you... in person I mean because I see you on Facebook all the time... I mean... not all the time because it's not like I'm stalking your profile or anything, but I... uh... see your photos and uh...' Chloe placed both hands on her head then sighed. 'I'm a nervous wreck. Can we start again?'

'Of course.' Willow laughed as she stood up. 'Hug?'

'Please.'

They hugged briefly then Willow stepped back to better look at Chloe. Her blonde hair was cut in a bob pushed back by oversized sunglasses and her eyes were the bright blue Willow remembered. She was wearing a green kaftan style dress with a denim jacket and green brogues. Her skin was pale apart from the colour in her cheeks and she looked good, but when they'd hugged Willow couldn't help noticing that Chloe had felt thin, fragile even in her embrace. Perhaps Chloe had been dieting or exercising a lot or perhaps it was just time or stress or ageing. Willow ate well and exercised regularly and though she was petite, she had curves that she was proud of. Her nan had always described her curves as *pear shaped* and that was fine with Willow, and Daniel didn't complain, in fact he seemed to adore her shape. Her thoughts strayed to that morning when they'd woken at six with the alarm and they'd... She shook herself inwardly. Now was not the time for remembering the passion she and Daniel shared.

Chloe was only two inches taller than Willow but growing up, it had often seemed more, especially when Chloe had worn platform heels on nights out. Willow hadn't been keen on heels, finding that she ended up walking like a nervous gazelle, but Chloe had been able to walk in them with the elegance of a catwalk model. Funny how different they had been in some ways and yet how similar in others.

'Shall we order then sit outside?' Chloe asked. 'It's such a beautiful day and I haven't been here in ages so I'd love to sit in the fresh air like we used to do. Besides which, at this time of the morning I'd normally be cooped up in a classroom with a bunch of teenagers so I'd really love to make the most of my current freedom.'

'Of course.' Willow nodded and they went to the counter and ordered coffees and cake then headed outside.

When they were seated at a table in the shade of a large old tree, Willow tucked her bag on the spare chair next to her and sat back.

'You look well, Chloe.'

'Thanks.' Chloe smiled. 'So do you.'

'Thanks.'

'Engaged life agrees with you.' Chloe took her sunglasses off her head and tucked her hair behind her ears then put the sunglasses back in her hair.

'I'm really happy. Daniel is an angel and I feel so lucky to have him in my life.'

'It's evident from the photos you post on Facebook how much you love each other.' Chloe lowered her gaze to the table and settled her hands there, lacing her fingers. 'How long have you been together now?'

Willow frowned. 'Gosh it's years. We were in our early twenties when we got together. Actually, I was twenty and Daniel was twenty-one. We met at university, remember.'

'Of course, I remember, but it was early days for you then and I wasn't sure it was serious at the time.'

'I thought we were just having fun at first but then years passed and we stayed together and now here we are. It seems such a long time ago now.'

'It is. But then time flies, right?'

A tiny line appeared between Chloe's brows and concern filled Willow's chest. Was Chloe happy?

'And how are you?' Willow asked. 'I know we exchange comments on posts sometimes on Facebook but it all seems so polite and... well... no one's going to pour out their reality over social media, are they?'

Chloe gave a wry laugh. 'Well... some people do but I know what you mean. I'm good, thanks. I'm still teaching, which is something I kind of fell into... as you know... but it pays the bills.'

'Do you enjoy it?'

'Sometimes.' Chloe shrugged. 'Some days are better than others but then the same can be said of every job, right?'

'That's true.' Willow thought of her own job as a family solicitor. Her days involved dealing with divorces and separations, custody arrangements, financial planning and more. She loved what she did but some days were certainly more interesting than others and her job did involve a high level of professionalism, a lot of patience and plenty of compassion. People's lives could be hard and Willow had always wanted to do what she could to help them through the difficult times. No one got married thinking it would end in divorce and Willow aimed never to judge anyone but to make her clients feel supported and safe when she worked with them.

'So you're still living in...' Willow fell quiet for a moment as a waitress delivered glass mugs containing their lattes and two slices of coffee and walnut cake. 'Thank you,' she said to the waitress – a young woman from the village called Verity Coombs.

'You're welcome. Let me know if you want anything else.' Verity flashed her a warm smile.

When Verity had gone, Willow reached for her latte and wrapped her hands around the glass. 'Reading, isn't it?'

'Yes. Been there since uni. I like the city life and the schools and the people. I'm happy there.' She picked up a fork and cut into her cake but Willow could tell that her old friend wasn't being entirely honest.

'You *are* happy there?' Willow prompted before taking a sip of her drink. It was warm, milky and delicious.

'Yes.' Chloe nodded, raising the fork to her mouth. She chewed and swallowed then went on, 'I rent a small flat not far from a park and some shops. There are plenty of pubs and cafés nearby too and there's lots to do.'

'Sounds great,' Willow said, thinking of how she'd hate to live anywhere other than near the sea where the skyline seemed endless and the air was fresh and clear. She could understand the allure of cities, of course she could, but living in one was never something she'd fancied. However, as long as Chloe was happy there, then that was all that mattered. 'So do you have a... I mean, are you in a...' She bit her lip, feeling bad for asking. Nothing said that Chloe *had* to be in a relationship.

'Am I seeing anyone?' Chloe put her fork down and picked up her latte. 'No. I've dated a bit but it's all so tiring and with work and everything...' She waved her hand vaguely and Willow wondered what *everything* meant. 'I just don't have that much free time.'

'I can imagine you must be very busy with teaching. I have the utmost admiration for teachers with the hours you put in and the dedication to the job that it requires.'

'Yeah...' Chloe sipped her coffee again then put the glass mug down. 'I'm actually doing supply teaching now. I was in a permanent job but I left... I wanted more freedom. As a supply teacher I still have some commitments, but if I stick to day-to-day work, it gives me far more flexibility.'

'To jet off to sunny climes on a whim?'

Chloe's eyes skirted around before settling on her plate again. 'Ha! Yeah...'

Willow might not have seen Chloe in person for a long time but she knew that look and it meant that Chloe was trying to avoid thinking about something. She didn't want to presume anything but she had her suspicions that Chloe wasn't as happy as she was trying to make out.

'Anyway...' Chloe leant forwards. 'Tell me how your nan is. I was so sorry to hear about her diagnosis.'

Willow gave a small nod, took a deep breath then proceeded to tell Chloe about her nan's cancer, how she'd declined further treatment and how they'd brought the wedding forwards so she could be there.

'That's a lovely thing to do,' Chloe said, her eyes red rimmed and shining. 'I always liked your nan.'

'She adored you and will be so excited to see you again.'

'Really?' Chloe reached into her bag and pulled out a tissue then dabbed at her eyes.

'Of course she will. She still talks about you all the time.'

'Oh...' Chloe's eyes filled with fresh tears and Willow reached across the table and took her hand. 'I'm so sorry, Chloe, I didn't mean to upset you.'

Chloe waved the tissue in front of her face. 'I'm... OK... I just... I missed her... and you... and...' She covered her eyes with the tissue and Willow gently squeezed her hand. It was like the years had rolled back and they were sitting here as teenagers putting the world to rights, discussing the latest chart songs, best family feud on EastEnders and whether ripped jeans were better than bootcut ones. They'd been so close back then and that was why Willow had known that if she did have just one bridesmaid, then it had to be Chloe. Willow had lots of friends but none of them went back as far as Chloe did and so when she walked down the aisle, she wanted Chloe there too. It had been something they'd planned as children and she couldn't envisage it any other way.

'We all missed you too,' Willow said. 'More than you'll ever know.'

They sat there quietly for a while, hands still joined, then they ate their cake and drank their coffees and Willow felt her guard lowering and the old sense of being comfortable around Chloe returning. There were things they didn't know about each other, and time had passed, but their bond was still there and she hoped they would be able to resurrect it in full, despite the more complicated reasons why they'd barely spoken for years.

Chloe

In the café toilet, Chloe splashed some cold water over her face then patted it dry with a paper towel. She met her eyes in the mirror and sighed. Getting upset at her reunion with Willow was not something she'd expected to happen but seeing her old friend again, hearing her familiar voice and feeling that Willow could see through her façade and understand exactly how Chloe had been feeling unsettled her. It brought a whole host of emotions to the surface and Chloe had been unable to push them back down.

Willow had once been her closest friend, the one person in the world aside from her mum and her nan, that Chloe had believed in and relied upon growing up. They'd shared so many secrets, hopes and dreams, had practically lived in each other's homes and seeing her again had brought home to Chloe exactly how much she had missed Willow.

And the talk about Barbara had been hard. Hearing first-hand how ill Barbara had been and about how she'd missed Chloe had twisted in her gut like a knife and she was over-whelmed with a yearning to see the elderly lady, hug her and apol-ogise for not being there all this time. Of course, it couldn't be that simple as other people were involved too, but Chloe hoped to see Barbara soon and to let her know that she had missed her.

But for now she would blow her nose, brush her hair then head back outside to where Willow was waiting for her because they were going to the local dress shop, *Sequins and Sandals*, to see if they could find something for Chloe to wear to the wedding. Willow had told her that due to the limited time available, she'd gone off the peg for her wedding dress and wanted the same for Chloe and it had been a relief. Chloe liked clothes but she wasn't keen on the idea of being measured, poked and prodded by a seamstress, so looking for a ready-made dress to wear would suit her just fine. *Sequins and Sandals* had been in the village since before Chloe and Willow were born, and was another family run business, but Willow had told Chloe that the owners had recently employed a fashion graduate named Rita Jolie who was renowned for creating the most fabulous fascinators and people had come from far and wide to purchase her creations. Willow was hoping that Rita would be able to provide her with something for the wedding because she didn't want to wear a traditional veil. It all sounded quite exciting to Chloe and she was looking forward to seeing what Rita would offer them.

Outside, Chloe found Willow waiting at the table where they'd had coffee and cake. The table had been cleared and Willow was putting her purse in her bag.

'How much do I owe you?' Chloe asked.

'It's my treat,' Willow said.

'No need.'

'Chloe, let me buy you a coffee for goodness' sake. You can get them next time if you like.'

'Sounds good to me.' And it did, the idea that she would be able to spend more time with Willow and to enjoy her company over coming weeks lifted her spirits. It brought home to her exactly how much she'd missed having a best friend over the years and how lonely she'd been, although admitting the latter was tough to do.

'Right then... shall we head over to *Sequins and Sandals*?' Willow asked.

'Definitely.'

They made their way along the path that led to the café and Chloe admired the rainbow of flowers in the borders and inhaled the sharp scent of the vibrant purple lavender in the stone pots at the gateway. While they walked, they chatted about the village and people they both knew, about those who were still here and those who'd left and Willow described new ones who'd moved to live in Sea Breeze Sands. It made Chloe feel sad that she had missed so much and yet it was also nice to catch up, plus the way Willow described some of the villagers made her laugh.

'How was it seeing your mum and gran?' Willow asked as they crossed the road and passed the row of shops that included the art gallery, baker, fish and chip shop and surf shop. She averted her gaze from the surf shop just in case she might happen to spot Theo through the window. She didn't feel ready to deal with seeing him right now.

'It was wonderful,' Chloe replied. 'Gran is just the same... fit as a fiddle and... oh goodness, I'm sorry.'

'What for?' Willow stopped walking and placed a hand on Chloe's arm.

'For saying that about my gran.'

'Why?' Willow knitted her brows.

'Well... because my gran is fit and healthy and your nan... isn't.'

'Oh Chloe, please don't worry about that. Honestly, I'm glad your gran is well. I'm devastated my nan is so poorly but that doesn't mean I want other people to suffer too. I love your gran, you know I do.'

'Thanks.' Chloe rubbed the back of her neck. 'I felt like an insensitive idiot then.'

'Well you're not so don't be daft.' Willow squeezed Chloe's arm then continued walking. 'What about your mum? Did she have lots to tell you?'

'She's... Well, she's the same but also different.'

'How so?'

'She's... dating someone and she seems to be quite loved up.'

'Really?' Willow glanced at Chloe, her eyebrows raised. 'Well that's good news.'

'Yeah...' Chloe thought about how it had felt when her mum had got home last night. It had been wonderful to see her but Chloe had also been surprised at how her mum had seemed to glow, as if something had been lit inside her and she was ablaze with happiness. 'It is good news. I'm happy for her.'

And she was. After all, her mum was only fifty and looked years younger. With her blonde locks and bohemian wardrobe, she seemed almost ageless and the glow that being in love had given her added to that effect. But Chloe had also felt a bit displaced by the knowledge that her mum had someone else. Not that she'd met him last night, but hearing her mum speak about him and relate what a fabulous evening she'd had was strange. After Chloe's dad had passed away when she was twelve, her mum had spent a long time alone and Chloe didn't want her to have to continue like that, but she'd also hoped to have some time with her mum and gran during her stay. Only now, she wasn't so sure she'd get that time with her mum, because she had spoken about how much she wanted Chloe to meet Carl Huxley, so she could see how amazing he was in person.

'Here we are then.' Willow opened the door of *Sequins and Sandals* and gestured for Chloe to go inside. 'Let's see if we can find something perfect for you.'

Chloe blinked as her eyes adjusted to the change in light. The interior of the shop was cool and smelt of vanilla and rose and Chloe realised it was coming from the reed diffuser on the table by the door.

'Good morning.' The voice came from across the shop where a shop assistant appeared to be wrestling with a naked woman.

'Morning, Rita.' Willow replied, gently nudging Chloe in the direction of the woman. 'Do you need a hand?'

Rita peered over the shoulder of what Chloe could now see

was a mannequin then disappeared behind it again. 'No thanks. I'm... nearly there.'

She set the mannequin upright in front of the counter then pointed at its lower half. 'Got some new bridal lingerie in so I was just popping the stockings on this one.'

'Oooh... very nice.' Willow peered at the lace topped white stockings. 'What do you think, Chloe?'

'Uhhh... nice,' Chloe said, though she'd never been fussy on stockings herself, finding them fiddly and uncomfortable.

'I think so and I'm sure Daniel would agree.' She giggled.

'We have quite a new range in stock, so while you're here I'll show you what we've got.' Rita bustled around the counter then started placing packages on the surface. 'They're suitable for bridesmaids too,' she said, and Chloe sighed inwardly. It seemed she wasn't going to get off that easily after all.

Theo

'What did you just say?' Theo shook his head as if in disbelief.

Willow chewed at her bottom lip then met his eyes. 'I invited Chloe for dinner.'

'But... what the... why ever... Why oh why *would* you do that?' Theo realised he was still shaking his head so he made an effort to stop.

'Theo, she's going to be my bridesmaid.'

'And?' He threw his hands up in the air then sighed. Willow had every right to invite Chloe for dinner but it had still come as a shock.

'It'll be nice to have some company.' Theo's mum smiled at him.

'Company? You have company in me, Willow and Daniel, Dad and Nan. Why do you need someone else?'

'Theo...' Willow placed a hand on his arm. 'Please put the potato peeler down so we can talk about this.'

Theo looked at his left hand that was wielding the potato peeler like a conductor's baton and laughed. His knuckles had gone white and the hand was noticeably trembling. He placed it on the kitchen worktop then wiped his hands on a towel.

'I met up with Chloe yesterday so we could catch-up and

choose a dress for her and we had a lovely time. She's going to be my bridesmaid and I don't want her to feel awkward on the day so I think it would be good for us all to spend some time together. I know that it's hard for you, especially, but that's why it seemed like a good idea to get it over and done with quickly. Like ripping off a plaster.'

'And you agree with this do you, Mum?' Theo asked.

'Willow did ask me what I thought and initially, I was concerned, but then we will all have to be in the same room again at the wedding so yes, I agree that this is a good way to break the ice.'

'The ice age you mean,' he muttered.

'Chloe doesn't seem as happy as I'd hoped she would be,' Willow said, her eyes widening meaningfully.

Theo's heart skipped a beat.

Chloe wasn't happy?

That wasn't how things were supposed to be. Chloe was meant to be a successful career woman, earning good money with a lovely home, several holidays a year and probably a handsome and wealthy partner who idolised her. Maybe even a child or two. That was why she'd left, to make a new life for herself away from Cornwall; that was why he'd watched her walk away, even though it had broken his heart, even though he'd wanted to beg her to stay.

'Did she tell you that?' he asked, averting his gaze from his sister to the bowl of potatoes so his she couldn't see his dismay.

'Not directly but I could see it in her eyes, hear it in her voice. I don't think things worked out the way she hoped they would.'

'Life often doesn't.' Theo pressed his lips together. This was not the time to get maudlin. Chloe was coming to dinner and so he'd plaster on a smile, welcome her back into the family home and make his best roast potatoes. Chloe had always liked his roast potatoes and they had never failed to make her smile. Perhaps today, he would see her smile again.

'Right then!' His mum clapped her hands. 'Chop! Chop!

Let's make a delicious dinner and show Chloe how happy we are to see her again. It will be difficult in some ways, Theo, I know, but a lot of time has passed and Chloe was always a part of this family. Obviously, we'd have liked things to work out differently all those years ago but it's in the past now. We need to focus on Nan, on the wedding and on moving forwards. Willow, can you slice and dice the carrots, please?'

'Of course.' Willow selected a knife from the block then started chopping.

Theo picked up the potato peeler again and got back to work. It would be challenging seeing Chloe, his glimpse of her at the beach had confirmed that for him, but it was inevitable that he'd see her over coming weeks anyway, so Willow was right; better to get it over and done with in the safety of the family home. He also knew that his nan would be delighted to see Chloe and that thought made it easier to deal with.

Willow

Willow wasn't completely insensitive. She knew it would be hard for Theo to see Chloe again. Theo had adored Chloe and years ago, they'd been inseparable, but now that she'd met up with Chloe, she knew her old friend hadn't changed that much and that she was still a warm and caring person. They'd had a great time the previous day, with Chloe trying on dresses, shoes and fascinators. Chloe had admired Willow's wedding dress, which had made Willow feel better about buying off the peg after years of swearing she'd have her wedding dress custom made. Chloe had settled on a dress herself and then they'd gone back to the café for lunch followed by a stroll along the beach.

It had been like old times being together again, laughing and joking, and Willow had felt very comfortable with Chloe. They knew each other well and though they'd not been in close contact for some time, they still had a bond that seemed unbreakable. Of course, Willow had some reservations about how Chloe had treated Theo in the past but she also knew that things had become complicated and that Chloe would have had her reasons. Plus, of course, she knew Theo well, and as much as she loved her brother even she could admit that he wasn't perfect. But then no one was and loving people was about accepting them, flaws and all.

Willow glanced across at Theo. Even though he was a man now, with his shiny brown hair flecked with some grey at the sides, stubble on his jaw, long hairy legs in comfy shorts and broad masculine shoulders, she could still see the little boy in him. He might be three years older than her but she'd always felt protective of him and wanted him to be happy. She knew losing Chloe had broken his heart and she never wanted to see that happen again, but she also knew that life went on and that spending time with Chloe again might give him some sort of closure. Chloe had disappeared so suddenly and so finally from his life that he'd been shocked at the time and Willow hoped that seeing Chloe again like this in a relaxed environment would help him to heal. Not that he hadn't done brilliantly over the years but there was no harm in helping things along. And, though she didn't want to admit it to herself, after seeing Chloe again yesterday, a part of Willow wondered if being together again might actually help Theo and Chloe realise what they were missing. It seemed that neither of them had fallen in love again and so surely that meant that they hadn't allowed themselves to let go enough to commit to someone else. Willow knew what it was like to love someone completely, to wake in the morning yearning for their touch and to think of them through the day, hoping that they were well and looking forward to seeing them. She couldn't begin to imagine what it would be like to lose Daniel and so her heart went out to Theo and to Chloe because even though Chloe had walked away from the relationship, knowing her as well as she had done, Willow had never been convinced that it was definitely what Chloe wanted. But she would never have presumed to try to change her mind, especially in light of the fact that she couldn't be objective because it had involved her brother too.

Chloe

'Hello, sweetheart.'

'Morning, Mum.'

Chloe crossed the kitchen, savouring the warmth of the floor tiles beneath her naked feet, the scent of croissants and coffee and the sight of her beautiful mum sitting in the window seat, legs stretched out, painted toenails, toe rings and ankle chains visible. She was wearing a violet silk kaftan with a green paisley print and her long hair was loosely pinned so that some tendrils curled around her neck. She could have been modelling for a bohemian clothing and accessories catalogue.

'There's coffee in the pot.' Her mum gestured at the worktop and Chloe nodded then helped herself to a mug.

Sitting on the edge of the window seat, she sipped her coffee then turned and gazed out of the window. The greenery of the land spread out in front of her and in the distance the sea glinted in the morning sunshine.

'It's a beautiful day,' she said.

'Perfect.' Her mum tucked her legs underneath her to make room for Chloe so she wriggled further onto the seat. 'Do you have plans?'

Chloe's stomach twisted. 'Yes. I'm... going to have dinner with Willow and her family.'

'With Willow's family?' Her mum's eyebrows rose a fraction.

'Yes.'

'I see.' Her mum raised her mug to her lips then lowered it and leant forwards, placing her free hand on Chloe's knee. 'How do you feel about that?'

'Honestly?'

'Of course.'

'A bit nervous.'

'About seeing all of them or seeing him?'

Chloe swallowed hard then sighed. 'All of them but mostly him. It's been a long time.'

'What is it about seeing him that's making you feel anxious?'

Her mum always did this, got right to the bottom of things and tried to make Chloe talk about them. She didn't always talk openly about her own feelings but had told Chloe many times that a problem shared was a problem halved, and so throughout her life, Chloe had tried to be honest with her mum. She knew there was no judgment from her mum or her gran and that did make talking to them both easier than talking to other people.

'I wonder how changed he'll be.'

'Physically or emotionally?'

'Both.' She gave a wry laugh. 'What if he looks really old?'

'What if he does?' Her mum gave a shrug. 'We all age.'

'Except you.'

'Ha! Even I'm ageing, Chloe.' Her mum ran a hand over her hair. 'I just hide the greys.'

'Mum, you look incredible. You always have done.'

'Being able to get older is a gift. Not everyone gets so lucky. I drink lots of water and wine,' she winked, 'eat well, moisturise daily and walk a lot in the fresh air, but apart from that, how I look is down to the good genes that Gran passed on. However, as I said, ageing is a gift and I'm grateful for every single day. I'm also very grateful that you've come home for a while. Gran and I miss you so much and we worry about you, so it'll be wonderful to spend time with you. Anyway... back to Theo. I can tell you now that I see him quite often and he has aged but in the good way that handsome men do. They improve like fine wine, if that helps, and Theo is a good vintage.'

Chloe smiled at her mum's teasing tone but her chest ached. 'I knew he'd look good but... that's not the important bit really. What if he's angry with me?'

Her mum pursed her lips. 'He might be... but then you could be angry with him. However, I suspect that any anger he felt will have cooled with time and that it will be nice for him to see you as it will be for you to see him. You were, after all, very good friends as well as being lovers.'

'Mum!'

'What? Chloe you were together for years. Of course you were lovers. Sex is a wonderful thing between two consenting adults and an important part of intimacy for many people.'

Chloe groaned inwardly, hoping her mum wasn't about to tell her about how great her *intimacy* was with her new boyfriend.

'Don't worry... I'm not about to tell you about my love life.' Her mum giggled. 'That's never something a daughter wants to hear.'

Chloe laughed. 'Thank goodness for that.'

'It's good to see you smiling. Do you feel a bit better now?'

'I do.'

'What're you going to wear?'

Chloe looked down at her pyjamas. 'I'm not sure.'

'I'd go smart casual if I were you. Look like you made an effort but didn't go mad.'

'Sounds good.' Chloe finished her coffee. 'Do you have plans today?'

'I thought I'd take a walk along the coastal path and sketch for a bit.'

'On your own?'

Her mum smiled. 'Yes, darling, Carl and I aren't joined at the hip.'

'Will you have dinner with Gran?'

'Absolutely! I wouldn't miss Gran's Sunday dinner for the world and a walk will work up an appetite too.'

'I'll eat with you this evening anyway.'

'Sunday evening cheese and wine.'

'Yum! I'll look forward to it.'

For as long as Chloe could remember, her gran and mum had enjoyed cheese and wine on Sunday evenings. After a large dinner, some cheese and crackers washed down with a good red wine was a lovely way to see out the weekend.

'Right, I'd better go and shower.'

'Remember... everything will be fine. It will be good for you to see Willow's family again because they did love you so much and I'm certain that Barbara will be over the moon.'

'They're good people.'

'They are.'

'Thanks, Mum.'

'Anytime, Chloe. That's what I'm here for.'

Chloe rinsed her mug in the sink then left the kitchen and climbed the stairs, hoping that she wouldn't get upset when she saw Barbara again and that Theo wouldn't be holding on to any residual anger because it was going to be difficult enough seeing him as it was.

Chloe

On the way to Theo's parents' house, Chloe battled her rising anxiety. It wasn't just about seeing Theo, it was seeing his family too. Once upon a time, they'd been like her extended family: lovely Lottie with her warm brown eyes and easy smile; Mike with his deep voice and protective instincts; Barbara with her quick wit and kindness, and Willow, the best friend she'd ever had. And then there was Theo, with his chocolate brown eyes, handsome face and the smile that had made Chloe's heart flutter. She had loved him deeply and yet, it hadn't been enough.

Why hadn't it been enough? What had she thought she was going to find when she left Sea Breeze Sands? Her priorities and outlook on life had changed since then, as had her understanding of the world. People were similar wherever you lived and having family and friends was what got you through the challenges. Chloe had felt lonely at times over the past eleven years. She'd had friends and colleagues, people she went out for the odd meal or drink with and had even dated a few times but there had been no one that she was as close to as she'd been to Theo and Willow. They had been her team, her tribe, and yet she had walked away from them both.

Spending time with Willow again had been lovely because

Willow didn't hate her, seemed to hold no resentment towards her and that had given her hope. If Willow could forgive her, then perhaps Theo could too.

And yet, she wondered, if she needed forgiveness. She'd been young back then, naïve, and had gone through an awful time. She'd experienced a loss that had rocked her, grieved for something that had barely even existed, for the way she had wanted things to be different. The way she'd behaved afterwards had been understandable to an extent and if it had been Willow going through what she had then she'd have supported her, been there for her and tried to help her through. No matter what. Willow had tried to be there for Chloe but she'd been torn between her best friend and her brother, dealing with her own sadness and trying to study for her degree. Willow had been under pressure too and so there was no way Chloe would blame her for anything. Instead, she had turned her anger on Theo because it was easier. If he'd been more exciting and adventurous then perhaps she wouldn't have felt the need to leave him and to change things. In retrospect, she could see that wasn't fair. Theo hadn't asked her to change, had loved her as she was and she should have done the same for him. That was something she would apologise for when she got the chance and for the way that she'd left; suddenly, ignoring his calls and texts, turning away from him as if he'd never existed. That had been her biggest mistake.

She reached the village green, admiring the trees that stood tall and verdant around the area, their leaves swaying in the gentle breeze. The sun was high in the sky and the morning was warm with the promise of a long and glorious summer. Chloe had missed the Sea Breeze Summers, the way that the village always looked so vibrant with an abundance of trees and flowers, shining windows and the fresh paintwork on houses and shops. The steady stream of tourists that flocked to the Cornish village could be fascinating, and as children, she and Willow had often made up backstories for the people they encountered, imagining that they were famous actors or band members with properties abroad and yachts moored out in the bay. They had dreamt that one day a successful movie director might spot them and ask them to feature in one of his films or a fashion designer might think them both beautiful and request that they model his latest range. Childish dreams, perhaps, but they had been fun and Chloe and Willow had revelled in the conversations that they shared on the beach, the coastal path, the café, and during the nights when they had sleepovers and midnight feasts.

Chloe pressed a hand to her chest. Remembering like this was bittersweet because she'd loved her childhood and its golden summers, especially the ones before they lost her dad and everything changed forever. Shaking her head, she pushed that particular sadness away. It was something she struggled to think about and so she rarely did. What was the point when dwelling wouldn't change what had happened?

She reached the large, detached house that overlooked the green and walked up the driveway. The hedgerow out front afforded privacy and the trees around the side provided shade in the summer and shelter in the winter. It was a house that had once felt like her second home and as she knocked on the front door, there was a tug at her heart as if it too was glad to return there.

Her stomach clenched at the sound of footsteps in the hallway and she tried to relax a bit, not wanting to grin at whoever answered the door like a demented ventriloquist's dummy. She adjusted her grip on the handles of the gift bag in her right hand, keen to avoid dropping the bag and smashing the bottle of wine or denting the box of chocolates that she'd picked up in the village grocery shop.

Then door swung open, and Chloe looked up...

Theo

His heart stuttered.

His mouth went dry.

His mind went blank.

Standing in the doorway, staring at Chloe like this was the strangest experience he'd ever had. It was weird because she looked the same and yet different. She still had hair the colour of sunshine, but it was shorter now, cropped into a neat bob. Her eyes were corn flour blue framed by fair lashes and brows. Her skin was pale but faint roses bloomed in her cheeks. Her face was still a perfect oval but her cheekbones were more prominent than he remembered. She was older and it had changed her slightly but not in a negative way. Theo had loved her when she was a young woman; now she was grown, her youthful softness had morphed into sharper edges and her eyes held knowledge and experience within them that hadn't been there before.

'Hello Theo,' she said, and the wooden floorboards seemed to quake under his feet. He placed a hand on the wall to steady himself.

'Hello Chloe.'

'This is for you all.' She held out a gift bag and he accepted it, peering inside to see wine and chocolates.

'Thanks. That's very kind of you.'

They stared at each other, eyes roaming hungrily.

There was a beat of silence. The air felt thick with tension.

The years of absence from each other's lives sat between them like a chasm full of curiosities.

'Excuse my poor manners,' he said, snapping himself out of his inertia, realising that they couldn't stand like this indefinitely. 'Please come in.'

He stepped back and Chloe entered the house bringing with her the scent of vanilla and amber, an aroma that stirred his soul.

'It's good to see you.' He closed the door. 'You look well.'

'So do you.'

Was this what it came to then? Two people who'd been lovers and best friends – who could kiss even when they had morning breath, who could break wind under the duvet and laugh about it – were now strangers, awkward, uncomfortable and shy. The sum of what they'd once been to each other was no longer a factor in their lives and so they didn't know how to act. It was simply awful.

'Go on through to the kitchen. Everyone's looking forward to seeing you.'

She glanced at him from under those pale lashes and said, 'Thanks.'

As she walked ahead of him, like she'd done so many times before, this time he didn't squeeze her shoulder or tug gently at her hair as he followed her.

This time, everything was different.

Chloe

Walking through the house was weird, like going back in time. Chloe had loved this house, she'd been happy when she'd spent time there and had felt as comfortable as in her own home. But it was also difficult being there, seeing how little it had changed over the years, except for a different shade of paint on the walls of the hallway, a different pot plant on the phone table, a mirror hanging on the wall that hadn't been there before.

The aroma of cooked dinner teased her nostrils and she realised that despite her nerves she was hungry. Theo's parents had always cooked a delicious Sunday lunch and Theo often helped out, becoming master of the roast potato. Chloe wondered if he'd made his famous roasties today and her mouth watered.

She paused in the kitchen doorway and glanced behind her at Theo. He gave her a thumbs up that she found both cute and encouraging.

'They can't wait to see you,' he said. 'It'll be OK, Chloe.'

She sucked in a shaky breath, grateful for the reassurance. He'd always been kind, always striven to reassure her, so the fact that he was still trying to do that, after everything, showed what a good human being he was.

The kitchen was bright and warm, and Chloe looked around, taking in the spacious kitchen diner leading on to a sunroom with bifold doors. It had been updated since she'd last seen it and she had to admit that the bifold doors, currently open so that the garden seemed like a part of the house, were a nice touch. The garden was vibrant with flowers in beds and pots and a perfect rectangle of grass at the centre – no doubt Mike's pride and joy. He'd always been a keen gardener and took pride in having an immaculate green lawn, something his wife had teased him about because she said it resembled a bowling green.

'Chloe!' It was Lottie, walking towards her, arms outstretched. She stopped when she was in front of Chloe and tilted her head. 'Sorry, I wasn't thinking heading towards you like that. Are we OK to hug?'

'Of course!' Chloe stepped forwards into Lottie's embrace.

'It's so good to see you, sweetheart.' Lottie murmured into Chloe's hair. 'We've all missed you so much.'

Chloe's vision blurred and she blinked the tears away, swallowed hard. 'It's good to see you too. Thanks for inviting me for lunch.'

'It's a pleasure.' Lottie stood back and gazed into Chloe's face. 'You've barely changed at all. Still pretty as a picture.'

'You look really good yourself.' Chloe smiled, though looking at Lottie she felt a twinge of concern. Lottie's face was pale, the lines around her brown eyes deep and long and her hair had gone completely grey. Clearly, worrying about her mum had taken its toll on her, as it would anyone who was worried about someone they loved.

'Mum will be delighted to see you. She's just woken from a nap and will be out once she's come round properly. She rests a lot these days.' Lottie's face fell for a moment then she seemed to shake herself and she straightened her back and brought her lips into a smile. 'Can I get you a drink? Wine? Coke? Tea?'

'Uhhh...' Chloe looked around to see what Theo's family were drinking but there was no one else in the kitchen yet.

'Let's have a glass of wine, shall we?' Lottie seemed to read her mind. 'It will help us relax a bit. I'm sure you're anxious about coming here today and I know that as much as I've been looking forward to seeing you, I've been anxious too.'

Chloe sighed shakily. 'I'm so sorry.'

'No, darling. Don't be.' Lottie took Chloe's right hand between both of hers. 'Don't be sorry. You're here now, you're going to be Willow's bridesmaid and it's wonderful to see you. We all missed you so please don't worry about anything else.'

'Thank you,' Chloe replied softly. 'I missed you too.'

'Mum?' Theo was standing in the doorway as if he'd been holding back to give them some space. 'Chloe brought wine and chocolates.' He held up the gift bag.

'How lovely! There was no need for you to do that but thank you, Chloe. Right, I have a zesty white in the fridge that's already cold, so I'll pour us a glass each of that then we can go and sit in the garden while Theo finishes making his roasties.'

'I was hoping he would.' Chloe started as the words left her lips. She hadn't meant to say that out loud.

'You were, eh?' Theo flashed her a cheeky grin then placed the gift bag on the work top. 'Some things don't change.'

Heat filled Chloe's cheeks and she was glad that Lottie was currently peering into the large American style fridge freezer. Blushing wasn't something she did often these days but then it had always been Theo who'd had the ability to make her blush. There were so many good things about him – his gentle teasing of her, the way he'd made her heart flutter and warmth emanate to her core, the way he'd known how to cheer her up when she was sad and the surprises he'd arrange like days out, picnics on the beach and champagne and strawberries in bed on her birthday – and Chloe had never met a man like him, never cared about anyone the way she cared for him. Theo was special, had a way of making her feel good, so why, then, had she left him behind?

She knew why and none of it had been simple at all.

'Here we are Chloe.' Lottie handed her a large glass that reminded her of a bowl. 'Cheers!'

They clinked glasses and when Chloe took a sip, the wine was light and delicious with a zest that seemed to fizz gently against her tongue. It warmed her stomach almost immediately and she knew she'd have to drink slowly to avoid getting tipsy.

'Let's go and sit outside for a bit. Everything's under control dinner wise and it's such a glorious day that it's a shame to waste it indoors.'

In the garden, they took seats at a table on the patio area. The air was filled with birdsong and the sweet fragrance of honey-suckle climbing the trellis on the garden fence. Chloe put her wine glass down and let the tranquillity of the garden wash over her, from the small water fountain in the rockery where the water was burbling away to the gentle hum of a lawnmower in a nearby garden and the full-throated warbling of a blackbird. The sky was flawless blue with just a few white puffs of cloud floating languidly along and a plane passing over, its contrail like a long powdery tail cutting through the blue.

'Is Willow here?' Chloe asked, realising she hadn't seen her friend.

'She was but she popped out to get something. Daniel's coming too so it'll be nice for everyone to catch up. Mike jumped in the shower just before you arrived because he was busy earlier making sure the garden looked 'just right' for your arrival. He'll be down shortly.'

'The garden is beautiful.' Chloe thought of Mike wanting to make things 'just right' for her and emotion swelled inside at that and at the knowledge that today would be just like old times: a full house, a Sunday lunch and a sunny Cornish day.

'So, Chloe... how have you been?' Lottie asked.

'Ummm...'

'I'm sorry. That's such a vague question, isn't it? I mean... it's been about eleven years, hasn't it, so I'm sure you've had good and bad days during that time. Goodness knows we have.' Lottie rolled her eyes then swigged her wine. 'Let me start again. Chloe, how are you *right now*?'

'I'm... OK, actually. I was, as you suggested earlier, anxious about coming here but it's wonderful to see you and to be here in your home. Meeting up with Willow for dress shopping was amazing. And... I have missed you all.'

'We missed you too. Very much. More than I can even begin to explain. But... how is Reading? Are you happy there?'

Happy? What constituted happy?

'I guess so.'

'That's not a clear answer.' Lottie leant closer. 'Do you have a house? Partner?'

'No to both.'

'You have a flat?'

'Kind of... I rent.'

Lottie raised an eyebrow. 'But no relationship?'

Chloe squirmed in her seat. Like Chloe's mum, Lottie had a way of getting straight to the heart of things. It wasn't that she was rude or nosey, but she cared and wanted to know exactly how people were feeling.

'No... No relationship.' Chloe shook her head.

'And now you're back in Sea Breeze Sands.' Lottie ran a finger around the rim of her glass. 'To stay?'

'I don't think so. I have a job in Reading...' *Not really, Chloe.* 'I mean... I work with a supply teaching agency.'

'So you could teach anywhere?' Lottie smiled.

'I guess so.'

Lottie nodded slowly as if digesting the information.

'Do you like teaching? I couldn't imagine dealing with teenagers all day every day. Being an accountant was hard enough and I worked with adults. Some didn't have a clue how to manage their accounts, mind you, but that's a whole other story.'

Chloe laughed at Lottie's comment. It wasn't the first time she'd heard about people Lottie had encountered over the years who didn't know where to start with record keeping. Not that

Lottie had ever named anyone because that would have been highly unprofessional, but she had shared some amusing anecdotes from time to time.

'I... I don't mind teaching. Mostly, the pupils are fine.'

'But is it your dream job?'

Chloe took a sip of wine to buy some time. 'I don't know. Actually... I do know and it's not. I'd still like to write, but... it seems like a dream, something that happens for other people and couldn't happen for me. I don't know if I'm diligent enough or talented enough to pull it off.'

Lottie pressed her lips together then steepled her hands on the table. 'You are an intelligent and capable woman, Chloe, and I'm certain you can do anything you put your mind to. I'm not sure why but you always lacked confidence and it saddened me. You should do what you want to do because I'm sure you'd be a brilliant writer and having dreams is important.'

Chloe filled her lungs with the sweet garden air and ran a finger through the condensation on the side of her glass. Sometimes it was good to hear what others thought about you because, as she knew, she often doubted herself and put obstacles in her own way. It would be possible to leave teaching, to come back to Sea Breeze Sands and stay with her mum and gran for a bit. She could take a breather, do some writing without worrying about letting the supply agency down, could walk on the beach and swim in the sea, and enjoy life for a bit while she figured some things out.

'You're very kind and wise, Lottie,' she said. *You always were,* she thought.

'Lottie?' The voice came from inside and Lottie jumped up as if she'd just been stung by a wasp.

'Coming!' She glanced at Chloe. 'It's Mum. I'll just go and help her outside.'

Chloe nodded but Lottie had already dashed away. No wonder she was looking a bit tired if she rushed around like that all the time. It couldn't be good for her.

A few minutes later, Lottie emerged with her arm supporting a tiny, frail woman. Chloe had to blink hard at the elderly woman so she could indeed confirm that it was Barbara Rees. She'd always been pleasantly plump and now she looked as though she was about six stone wet through. Her glasses seemed too large for her face and her short wispy hair stuck up like wire wool.

'There she is,' Barbara said, as she lowered into the chair Lottie had pulled out for her. 'My sweet, beautiful girl.'

'Hi,' Chloe forced out through trembling lips. She'd tried to prepare herself for seeing Barbara, but it was still a shock. It hit her then how many years she'd been away and how some things had changed beyond recognition.

'Here you are, Nan.' It was Theo with a furry throw that he tucked in around his grandmother, in spite of the warmth of the day, before kissing her forehead. 'I'll get your mint tea now.'

'You're an angel, Theo.'

Lottie sat down again but seemed tense now, as if she'd spring from her seat at any moment.

'Oh do relax, Lottie.' Barbara coughed. 'You're making Chloe and me feel tense sitting like that. I'm fine, my darling, I promise you. It's simply wonderful to be outside.'

'I just worry about you getting cold, Mum.' Lottie sat back in her chair but the tendons in her neck were protruding so Chloe knew she wasn't relaxed.

'It's a sunny day, Lottie. I'm not going to catch cold out here so stop worrying. Drink some more of that wine. It'll do you good.'

Lottie nodded and lifted her glass but she barely took a sip before she lowered it again. 'We could go and sit in the lounge. There are no drafts in there.'

'Lottie!' This time Barbara's tone was sharp. 'Please stop fretting. I know you love me and want the best for me but I would like to stay out here. The honeysuckle smells incredible and I love listening to the birds. I spend plenty of time indoors so this is a welcome change.'

'OK.' Lottie's eyes flickered from her mum to Chloe, and she could see the angst there. Poor Lottie must be exhausted with worry.

'Well, Chloe.' Barbara turned her curious gaze to Chloe. 'It's absolutely wonderful to see you although I have to be honest, you're looking a bit skinny for my liking.'

'Ditto.' Chloe winced at her reply. 'Oh... I'm so sorry, I didn't mean to say that then. It just slipped out and—'

But Barbara was chuckling. 'Don't sweat it, Chloe. Ha! Ha! It's refreshing to have someone speak directly to me. Even the doctors whisper in corners and send meaningful glances Lottie's way, as if they think the truth about this damned disease inside me will kill me. I know the score... The disease itself is doing the damage not the truth about it. I'm on my way out but I'm still human. I haven't lost my wits or my hearing and I can tell when someone is trying to hide behind euphemisms. Thank you for being honest with me. I know I look a state. My Bill would have a fit if he saw me so in way I'm glad he went first. When I was younger, I was always insisting that I needed to go on a diet but he'd dismiss my plans and tell me he liked my curves exactly the way they were. He said he didn't want to cuddle up to a skeleton at night because how would that be pleasant?' She laughed but the laughter turned into coughing that wracked her tiny frame. 'I'm all right,' she said finally, sitting upright and accepting the mug of tea Theo had brought her. He paused for a moment but Barbara waved a hand at him so he headed inside, muttering something about turning the roasties. 'I just... needed a drink.'

When some colour had returned to Barbara's cheeks, she smiled at Chloe. 'As I was saying... you look a bit thin and so do I. However, I know why I'm this way but what about you? Are you on a diet or something?'

Chloe shook her head. 'No, not at all. I'm just really busy with work and life.'

'In Reading?'

'Yes.'

'She teaches, Mum, remember?'

'Of course I remember, Lottie. Willow told us recently.'

'She did. I'm sorry, I'm quite forgetful these days.' Lottie suddenly drained her wine glass then stood up. 'I'll go and get some more wine.'

When Chloe and Barbara were alone together, Barbara said, 'She worries so much and I know this is hard for her.'

'She loves you,' Chloe said.

'She does and I love her too but she doesn't half fuss around me. Between you and me, it's a bit suffocating at times. I understand how difficult this is for her but sometimes... I feel guilty for having cancer.'

'What? But that's not your fault.'

'The rational side of me knows that but the part of me that wakes in the early hours and makes my heart race feels guilty. If I wasn't ill, then Lottie wouldn't be going through this and neither would the rest of my family.'

'People go through this all the time, though, and no one would ask to have cancer. I'm so sorry that you have it, Barbara.'

'Me too, but what are you going to do, eh? I'm eighty-four and I've had a good life. I wouldn't have minded another decade but then I see those adverts with the poor children who have cancer and I know how lucky I've been. I've lived a long time and it's been bloody brilliant. However, one of my last wishes before I go was to see you again and it has come true!'

A tear escaped Chloe's eye and rolled down her cheek. She wiped it away with the back of her hand, battling with the ache in her throat. Barbara was being so brave, seemed so stoic about her diagnosis and Chloe wasn't surprised at all; Theo's grandmother had always been the same. But it did seem unfair that Barbara and her family had to go through this and Chloe wished there was something she could do to help.

'Chloe, don't be sad. I'm OK, I promise you. I've made my peace with it and I'm going to get to see Willow getting married and what a send-off that will be. I wish...' she said, a crafty expression on her face, 'that I could have seen Theo married too... or at least happily settled... but perhaps that's too much to ask for. Unless, of course, you and Theo realise how much you still care for each other and get back together. Ahhh... if only... then I could die happy.'

Just then, Chloe noticed Theo in the doorway and from the way his eyes had widened, she suspected he'd heard what Barbara said. Chloe looked down and feigned interest in her cuticles, not wanting to look into Barbara's questioning gaze or over at Theo. Did Barbara really think there was a chance of her and Theo getting back together or was she teasing? It could be that she wasn't as sharp as usual, that pain medication or even the worry of her diagnosis was affecting her mentally and emotionally. But she had said that knowing that Chloe and Theo were back together would allow her to die happy.

What if they could give her that?

Chloe raised her eyes and found Theo's gaze fixed on her face, his expression thoughtful, as if he was thinking the same as her.

He cleared his throat as if to announce himself to his nan then came out to them. 'Willow and Daniel have arrived and Dad's opening some more wine. Plus... dinner is ready so let's get you inside, Nan, so we can eat.'

'Yes, darling,' Barbara said, as Theo helped her up.

'I'll bring the mug,' Chloe said as she picked up Barbara's tea and her wine glass, and followed Theo and Barbara inside. They walked very slowly, more of a shuffle than a walk, but Chloe was happy to follow them. It gave her a chance to compose herself before being reunited with everyone again.

So far, the day had been positive and she hoped it would continue that way, although what Barbara had said had struck a chord with her and she wondered if Theo was feeling the same way too.

Theo

Sitting at the kitchen table surrounded by chatter and laughter, the clinking of cutlery and the aromas of beef and roast potatoes, Yorkshire puddings and a variety of vegetables, Theo could almost believe he'd gone back in time. This was a regular occurrence at his parents' home, but today Chloe was with them again, and things were as he'd once imagined they would be.

He sipped his wine then looked around the table, feeling pleased to see his nan smiling. Chloe's presence had definitely changed something in his nan for the better. It was as if Chloe had brought her back and she was more 'herself' than she had been recently. He could see from the way his nan occasionally closed her eyes or bit her bottom lip, that the pain was there – even with meds it could never be completely erased – and she'd barely touched her food, but the way she smiled at Chloe and touched her hand from time to time revealed her delight. He sent a silent thank you to Willow for asking Chloe to be her bridesmaid. It had been a good move, one that was helping their grandmother and one that he could appreciate. Over the years, he'd doubted himself and his past decisions, had wondered if Chloe really had been the incredible person he'd thought she was. But seeing her again and watching her interact with his family confirmed that she was a good person, was kind and compassionate, fitted in with his family, and seemed comfortable there.

He knew it would've been hard for Chloe coming back but she'd done it and she was clearly making an effort to speak to everyone at the table. She'd always got on with his family, but again, during her years away, he'd come to believe that he must have imagined how well she fitted in with them. Now he knew that he hadn't imagined it and that Chloe was who he'd believed her to be. There was just the end of their relationship to contend with and that still didn't sit well with him. How could it when it had caused so much pain and confusion?

But right now, there was no point dwelling on that. It would serve no purpose other than to anger him or to rake up the old ache of loss. Besides which, he had something else to consider. He'd overheard his nan telling Chloe she was happy she'd see Willow married before she passed away and then she'd said she wished she could see Theo settled too. *With Chloe.* He knew his nan was intelligent and could be wily but wasn't sure if she was serious about this or if she was teasing them. But why would she? She'd been hurt when Chloe had left their lives too but she'd tried to understand, had even told Theo that sometimes people had to walk away from their loved ones and that if what Chloe felt for Theo was genuine and meant to be then she'd be back. Years had passed and she hadn't returned. *Until now.*

Perhaps it was fate. Perhaps Chloe was always going to come home at some point and realise how much she still loved him.

He gave himself a mental shake. That was ridiculous. Theo wasn't a believer in fate and all that nonsense. Of course it would be nice to have faith in something like that, to believe that it was inevitable that Chloe would return because they were meant to be together, but this wasn't a Hollywood romcom and things like that didn't happen in real life.

Just then, Chloe giggled loudly at something his dad had said and Theo found himself smiling at how she threw back her head, all self-consciousness gone in the moment of amusement. As if sensing his eyes on her, she looked straight at him and smiled. Heat shot through him like an electric shock, awakening parts that he'd long since shut down, knocking down the sturdy walls he'd erected around his fragile heart.

That look. Those piercing blue eyes. That hair like a halo, ruffled now from where she'd dragged her hand through it to push it back from her face.

This was Chloe. The woman he'd loved and adored. The woman he'd thought he'd spend his life with. She was here. Right now. *Here.*

When she broke eye contact, he almost groaned out loud, but then he noticed how his nan was gazing at Chloe as if she was an angel come to earth. And he knew then what he needed to do. Chloe might not agree to it, but he had to try.

For his nan's sake, he would ask Chloe to pretend they were back together. It would delight his nan if they were able to grant her this one last wish.

Willow

Willow's face was aching from smiling so much. She'd thought that having Chloe over for lunch would be challenging but better done now than closer to the wedding, but she hadn't expected it to go as well as it had. Her family had accepted Chloe as easily as they used to do, as if she had never gone away. They'd been warm and courteous, funny and friendly and lunch had been wonderful. Willow had eaten too much, especially too many of Theo's roast potatoes considering she had a wedding dress to fit into, but she had enjoyed every mouthful.

At her side, Daniel was sitting back in his chair, nodding at something her dad was saying. Her heart filled with love for the two men, her rocks, the man who had raised her and the one who would soon be her husband. Whenever she thought that, her stomach flipped. Daniel would be her husband and she couldn't wait for that day. Her own feelings also made her conscious of something else that was fizzing in the room. She'd noticed the looks shared by Chloe and Theo as well as the ones they cast each other's way when they thought the other was unaware. If she was reading things right, there was still a spark between the two of them and she wondered if it was something real that could last or if it was nostalgia and would soon be forgotten when Chloe went back to her life in Reading. Willow knew that Theo had never fallen in love after Chloe, that he'd been unable to give himself to another and that his heart had never fully repaired.

But was that because he still had feelings for Chloe?

Did he still love her?

Willow's eyes strayed to her nan and she smiled inwardly. Barbara was enjoying herself, chatting to Chloe every now and then, reaching for her hand, gazing at her adoringly. Chloe was, even after the years that had passed, a part of the family and it seemed that nothing – not time, distance or past heartbreak – was going to change that.

'Right,' Theo said as he stood up, 'I'm going to clear the table then get dessert.'

'I don't think I could eat another thing.' Chloe pointed at her softly rounded stomach. 'I'm fit to burst.'

'Nonsense.' It was Willow's dad. 'You need some meat on your bones, Chloe.'

'I agree.' Willow's nan was grinning at Chloe. 'Have some dessert for me, Chloe because I can't face any.'

'Won't you try a little bit, Barbara?' Chloe asked.

'I don't think so, my darling.'

'How about some ice cream, Nan, or some sorbet?' Theo asked. 'One scoop?'

Barbara pouted then inclined her head. 'Go on then. Just one small scoop of lemon sorbet to clear my palette.'

'That's the spirit.' Theo picked up some plates and carried them to the sink.

'I'll help.' Chloe jumped up and started clearing the table. Willow's mum was about to get up but Willow placed a hand on her arm and gave a brief shake of her head. It would do Chloe and Theo good to have a few moments away from them all, even if they were only on the other side of the room. She had a feeling that Theo had something he wanted to say to Chloe and this would give them that opportunity.

'Uhhh... Darnit. I think the sorbet is in the garage freezer,' Theo said theatrically. 'Chloe... fancy coming to check?'

Willow almost rolled her eyes but Theo had never been a good actor. He wore his heart on his sleeve and it was, she thought, one of the things that made him such a sweet and special guy. Though curiosity burned through her about what Theo wanted to say to Chloe, she forced herself to sit still and to tune back into the story her dad was telling Daniel. There would be time enough to find out what was going on and she'd have the chance to speak to her brother later.

'What is it, Mum?' Lottie pushed her chair back and went to her mum's side, alarm etched on her features.

'Don't look so worried, Lottie. I just need a wee.'

'Of course.' Lottie cast a relieved glance at Willow then helped her mum get up from her seat. 'Let's get you to the toilet.'

'I shouldn't have drunk so much mint tea.' Willow's nan winked at her as she passed. 'Makes me like a leaky tap, it does.'

'It's good for you, Barbara. It's very important to stay hydrated,' Willow's dad said.

'I know. I know. But you try going for twenty billion wees a day. I'm sure you'd get fed up too, Mike.'

Willow's dad laughed and she joined in. If they could laugh, even when things were as serious as they were with her nan, then at least they could ease the tension. Having Chloe there today had made things feel a bit more normal and Willow was grateful for her company. Having her there made it feel like their family was complete again and she wondered if everyone felt the same way.

Chloe

Chloe followed Theo out to the garage and waited while he searched through the chest freezer. He pulled out two tubs of sorbet and held them up.

'Lemon and raspberry. Something to tempt Nan.'

'She'll be pleased.' Chloe watched him carefully. Had he really brought her out here to talk about sorbet?

'Chloe,' he said, closing the freezer and placing the tubs on the lid. 'It's good to see you.'

'Likewise.'

'Thanks for coming over for lunch. As you can see, you've really made Nan's day.'

'I'm glad to have the chance to spend some time with her.'

'I can't believe she's so poorly.' His Adam's apple bobbed. 'I mean... she's always been the heart of the family. She's the one who's there for us all, offering advice and hugs, helping us to work things out. And now...' He dropped his gaze to the concrete floor.

Chloe stepped closer to him and touched his arm. 'I'm so sorry, Theo. I can hardly believe she's not well even though I've seen her now. She was always the wise grandmother, strong and resilient, and I thought she'd be around forever.'

He looked up and held her gaze. 'I wish she could be. I don't want her to suffer but I don't want to lose her either.' He rubbed at his temples as if he had a headache and closed his eyes. His chest rose and fell slowly as he took slow deep breaths and Chloe suspected that he was trying to control his emotions.

'If there's anything I can do, Theo. Anything at all.'

His eyes snapped open. 'Actually, Chloe, there is something.'

'Go on.'

'We don't know how long Nan has left and... see... she loves you. She's always loved you. And she's worried about me. She told me the other day that it would make her happy to see me settled too, like Willow. Since you...' His cheeks flushed. 'There hasn't really been anyone. Not that I've been a monk.' He gave wry laugh. 'But I just didn't find someone I wanted to be with. After Nan told me that she wanted to see me settled down, I thought about how easy it would be to help her with that. You know?'

Chloe swallowed hard. What was he asking her? 'You want to... get back together?'

His brown eyes were so dark they seemed to liquify and Chloe felt unsteady on her feet. She placed a hand on the freezer lid to ground herself. A memory pierced her mind: she was out here with Theo when she was sixteen and he was nineteen. They'd made the excuse that they wanted to get something from the freezer so they could steal a few moments alone. Theo reached for her as soon as they closed the garage door behind them then gazed into her eyes before lowering his head to hers. A year or so later, the same thing, a regular occurrence after Sunday lunch. Theo holding her so tight she felt she couldn't catch her breath and then, as his mouth met hers, feeling like the world was spinning as love and desire collided. Even when she'd return from university, their longing for each other would be unquenchable and they'd kiss and hug, make love every chance they got. *So much passion. So much love.*

'Chloe...' Theo reached for her now, placed his hand on her

arm, and her skin tingled in ways it hadn't done for years. He was so close she could feel the warmth from his body, smell his spicey, woody cologne, kiss him if she stepped forwards and raised her head. Her heart pounded and she exhaled a shaky breath.

'Theo?'

A thousand things emerged with her question, and she wondered if he understood.

'Will you... will you help me make Nan happy, Choe, by pretending that we're back together?'

'Back together?'

'Yes.'

Chloe frowned and took a step back. Why was this all so confusing? Theo wasn't asking her to get back with him. That would be ridiculous. Instead, he was asking her to act as if they were a couple again for his nan's sake. To make her happy during her final months or weeks or days. Chloe cared about Barbara, seeing her again had brought her love for the elderly lady and her family rushing back, and so of course Chloe would do what she could to help.

'Anything.' She inclined her head. 'Anything to help.'

Relief swept over his features and Chloe raised a hand, touched his cheek, gasped at the spark that shot through her and warmed her heart.

Theo covered her hand with his and smiled, his eyes glistening. 'Thank you so much, Chloe. You don't know how much this means. It's a big ask, I know, and I wouldn't have even considered it but I want to do this one last thing for Nan.'

'I love Barbara and want to help too. But...' She paused as something occurred to her. 'What about everyone else? How do we get around that? It would be unfair to deceive your family and mine.'

'We'll speak to them discretely about it and explain that we're doing it for Nan's sake. They'll understand and then they won't be disappointed afterwards when we—' Pain clouded his eyes. 'That sounded so callous... saying *afterwards*...'

'I knew what you meant. Be kind to yourself now. This is a good thing.'

He nodded but his eyes were moist and Chloe couldn't help herself. Instinct took over and she slid her arms around his waist and hugged him. He froze, arms at his sides, and she felt the thud of his heart, a powerful drum beat, beneath her cheek. Then, slowly, his hands moved around her waist and he hugged her back, resting his chin on the top of her head.

He smelt familiar, felt familiar and yet so different. Since they had last hugged, Theo had changed from the slim young man he'd been into a muscular, broad shouldered man in his thirties. His body was hard, his hands strong as they held her. Chloe had missed this, the touch and presence of another human being; the warmth and reassurance of another body against hers; the scent and essence of Theo.

When he released her, she almost sighed with disappointment, but Theo placed a finger under her chin and raised it gently. 'Will you be OK with... acting?'

'Acting?'

'You know... being tactile and... things in front of Nan?'

Chloe smiled in spite of the whirlwind of emotions inside her. 'I think I can manage it.'

'Good.' He returned her smile. 'As long as you're OK with that.'

'We'd better get that sorbet inside before it melts.' Chloe smoothed down her hair and reached for a tub of sorbet.

'I guess we'd better.' Theo chuckled softly.

As they made their way back inside, Chloe couldn't help wondering if they were doing the right thing, or if this would make things difficult for them both.

She hadn't expected to end up in Theo's arms or to feel everything she just had and if they had to keep up the pretence of being together for the foreseeable future, then what effect would that have upon her and her feelings for the man she'd once loved with all her heart?

Theo

It was only just after seven, but the excitement of the day had tired Theo's nan and he'd been glad to sit with her and read aloud until she drifted off. She looked like a tiny china doll in her floral print nightdress, the double bed seeming enormous around her. He stood up quietly and tucked the covers around her then gently kissed her forehead. Her eyelids flickered but she didn't stir, so he turned off the lamp and crept from the room.

He pulled the door behind him, leaving it open a crack in case she called out for anyone. It was strange how things changed as people aged, he thought. It didn't seem that long ago that his nan was reading him bedtime stories and tucking him into bed when he spent the night at her house or when she babysat for him and Willow. In reality, it was years ago, but the older he got, the more he was conscious of how quickly time seemed to pass.

'You OK?' Willow was making coffee in the kitchen.

'Yeah.' He walked over to and got a mug out of the cupboard. 'Can I have one?'

'Of course you can.'

Willow made an extra coffee then handed it to him. 'You want to talk?'

'Shall we sit outside?' He nodded at their nan's door, making it clear that he didn't want to disturb her.

'I'll just take these through to Mum and Dad then I'll join you.' Willow picked up two mugs and took them through to the lounge where their parents were watching TV. Daniel had gone home earlier to get some ironing done for the week, but Willow had stayed to spend time with her family. Chloe had left not long after Daniel, and Theo could tell that it wasn't easy for her to leave. It was as if now that she'd been reunited with Theo's family, she wanted to make up for lost time.

Theo let himself outside then took a chair at the patio table. He placed his mug in front of him and leant his elbows on the table, his chin on his hands.

He'd seen Chloe to the door earlier, had faltered as they said goodbye, wondering if he should hug her again. They hadn't resurrected their relationship immediately over dinner – or should that be their *fake* relationship – because they didn't want to arouse his nan's suspicions, but they'd spoken about it on the doorstep and agreed to do so gradually so it seemed natural. Then they'd exchanged numbers so they could stay in touch.

Theo had offered to walk her home but she'd laughed and waved a hand at him, telling him that she'd be fine. It had gone against his instincts to let her walk home alone – he wasn't sure these days if being a traditional gentleman was politically correct, but he'd always want to display good manners and ensure that he did what he could to ensure that the women in his life were safe. But as he'd watched her walking away, he'd reasoned with himself that Sea Breeze Sands was a safe location, it was still light and Chloe knew her way home. She'd also lived in Reading for the past decade and was perfectly capable of taking care of herself. It was just that things that had lain dormant inside him during her absence from his life seemed to want to raise their heads again now that she was back, making him want to be there for Chloe as he once had been.

When Chloe was out of sight, he'd closed the door and gone

back inside, wishing he'd asked her to text him when she'd got home to let him know she was OK, hoping she would do.

He picked up his mug and sipped his coffee, watching a small bird as it hopped around the grass. If his dad could see it he'd shoo it away, not wanting his flawless lawn ruined by a bird looking for worms, but Theo liked watching the bird. It was determined and diligent and sooner or later, it would find whatever it was that it was searching for.

The sky was golden now, laced with pinky-purple hues and the air was fragrant with the scent of roses. Somewhere in the distance a dog barked and another one answered it. Sea Breeze Sands was the same as always but knowing that Chloe was there too, under that same patch of sky, made it even better.

'Right then,' Willow said, as she sat down, dragging him from his thoughts. 'What's going on?' She fixed her emerald eyes on him and ran a hand through her raven black hair, sweeping it forwards so it fell over one shoulder.

'I had a good day,' he said evasively. 'Did you?'

'I had a lovely day but there's something going on and I want to know what it is.' She cocked an eyebrow at him. 'You and Chloe disappeared to the garage then you came back and something had changed.'

'What do you mean? In what way?'

'It was like the atmosphere between you was charged.'

Theo chewed at his lip. 'Really?'

'Yes, really. So what happened between you?'

'Nothing.' He laughed. 'Nothing at all.'

'Liar!' Willow leant forwards. 'Don't forget I know you well, big brother.'

'OK. OK... Chloe and I talked and decided that we want Nan to be happy.'

'We all do.'

'Exactly. She's told me more than once that it would make her happy to see me settled too.'

'What, married?'

He shrugged. 'In a relationship, at least.'

'She has said that.' Willow gave a brief nod. 'So what's the plan?'

'Chloe and I are going to pretend that we're back together.' He watched his sister's eyebrows raise. 'Just until... you know... so Nan will stop worrying about me.'

'I hear you.' She sighed. 'But what about Mum and Dad? Don't you think they'll worry if you and Chloe are an item again? After the last time, they'll be terrified of seeing you hurt and they're already going through enough as it is.'

Theo was shaking his head. 'Everyone will know the truth.'

'Except for Nan?'

'That's right.'

Willow sat back and tapped a fingertip against her mouth. Theo waited, knowing she'd need time to digest what he'd told her. 'And Chloe's OK with this?'

'She said she is.'

'I like the idea of making Nan happy but I am worried about you and about Chloe. Won't this be hard on you both? I mean... you were in love and very close for a long time. What if one of you gets keen again and ends up hurt? Even if it's just a pretend relationship, old feeling might rise to the surface and it could cause pain.'

'It could. But Chloe and I are both adults. We've discussed it and feel that it's a good thing to do for Nan.'

'I can see how it would make her last weeks—' Willow slapped a hand to her mouth, eyes wide with shock. 'I hate saying that. I hate even thinking it.'

'I know. I do too but we need to face reality. Nan doesn't have long left and this would make her happy. She loves Chloe and would be over the moon to see us as a couple. I'm sure I'm capable of pretending for a while without getting emotionally involved.'

He gritted his teeth together, wondering if he was telling the truth or what Willow wanted to hear.

'OK.' Willow picked up her mug and sipped her coffee. 'As long as you're both going into it with your eyes open and you speak to Mum and Dad and to Chloe's family. That way, no one will be confused or hurt when you're not really together after... well, you know.'

'Will do.'

'You'll have to dance with her at the wedding and hug her... perhaps kiss her.' Willow twirled a few strands of her hair. 'Won't that be challenging?'

Theo thought of how it had been to hold Chloe earlier that day, to feel her body against his, to smell her hair and her heady perfume, to almost kiss her as a passion he'd long since buried rose to the surface, taking him by surprise.

Yes, it would be challenging.

Yes, it would be risky.

But it was a risk he was willing to take because it would make one frail, elderly lady very happy indeed.

Chloe

'Have another glass!' Willow waved the bottle of champagne in the air.

'I'm fine, honestly.' Chloe held up her full champagne flute. She was pacing herself, not wanting to get drunk on Willow's hen night and make a fool of herself. Afterall, they weren't teenagers or twenty-somethings anymore when getting tipsy or even drunk had seemed acceptable. Besides which, Chloe had to get herself home at the end of the evening and possibly Willow too, so she'd keep her wits about her and be the sensible one.

'Get it down you.' Willow sashayed away, her hips swaying in time to the music, then she proceeded to fill the glasses of the other women who'd joined them for her hen night.

Chloe wandered over to the French doors that led out to the garden of The White Horse. The pub was Saturday evening busy with music playing in the bar where the hen night was, the TV screen flashing in the lounge where locals were watching the sports channel and plenty of people coming and going.

Chloe leant against the open door and gazed into the garden. A squirrel raced across the grass then up a tree where it disappeared into the branches. The air was heady with the sweet fragrance of the roses climbing the exterior of the old stone building and the sky was indigo peppered with lavender streaks, the stars just beginning to appear.

Two weeks had passed since she'd had dinner with Theo's family and she'd thought of little else. It was strange how she'd pushed all thoughts of Theo and his family away for years and suddenly, they were in her mind, filling her dreams, and she felt like she was losing control of something she'd tried to manage for years. Her feelings for Theo had been deep and complex, but she'd been so young back then and so had he. Now they were older, hopefully wiser, and Chloe had learnt a lot over the years about life and how sometimes what you thought you needed and wanted wasn't that great after all. Love, when you found it, was to be treasured and Chloe had never loved a man in the way she'd loved Theo.

She stepped outside and kicked off her sandals then walked across the grass and sat on the bench underneath the shade of an old oak tree. The breeze gently rustled the leaves and she placed a hand against the bark, feeling the rough texture beneath her palm, the strength of this living thing that had grown in this spot for centuries. In light of that, her own problems seemed so small and insignificant. Life was fleeting for human beings, the years flew past, but she'd always believed that love could last a lifetime and beyond. People could continue through their loved ones, their children and grandchildren and so they never really disappeared altogether.

She leant backwards and peered around the thick trunk, and there it was. Etched into the bark, the letters TT loves CR forever. *Theo Treharne loves Chloe Redgrave forever.* Theo had carved that into the bark years ago when they'd first started dating. They'd been out here one summer's evening, kissing and cuddling on this very bench, and Theo had told her that he'd love her forever. Giggling, Chloe had told him to prove it, and so he'd gone to the bar and got a corkscrew, then brought it outside and carved his love into the tree.

She ran a fingertip over the carving, thinking of how innocent they'd been back then, of how they'd believed that their love would endure and that they'd always be together. It was good that they'd been innocent and unaware of what lay ahead, she thought now. Not all young people were so lucky, obviously, but Chloe and Theo had been. They'd had families that loved them, each other and they'd enjoyed many happy times.

What if Chloe had stayed in Sea Breeze Sands? Would they still have been together, sat out here together and admired Theo's graffiti? Shown it to their children? One day to grandchildren?

She took a gulp of champagne, needing some courage to deal with her thoughts. Coming back to the village was bound to have stirred up her emotions. The whole place had memories at every turn and while most of them were good, it still hurt to remember what had gone wrong.

But now she and Theo were pretending to be a couple again. They'd only met briefly over the past fortnight when she'd gone to his parents' house to spend time with him and Barbara, and they hadn't been alone at all. They'd decided to take it slowly in terms of seeming to get back together and so they'd shared some lingering glances that had made Barbara smile but they didn't want to overdo things and arouse her suspicions. There was no point in pretending to be back together unless they did it convincingly. However, now that the wedding was just three weeks away they'd decided to step up the pace and they would make it clear to Barbara that they were dating again.

The thought made Chloe's stomach flip over like she'd just jumped off a cliff. It was a big thing to do and she worried that she might not be convincing but then, whenever she saw Theo and gazed into his eyes, the doubts disappeared like smoke on the breeze and it was all she could do not to launch herself into his arms again for one of his hugs.

Swallowing down the rest of her champagne, she pushed herself to her feet and fluffed her softly waved hair. She'd made an effort with her appearance this evening and she was, in reality, here for Willow. Therefore, sitting outside moping was unfair of her, especially seeing as how she was the sole bridesmaid. She could, surely, enjoy a few drinks and have some fun for Willow's sake.

She plastered on a smile then headed back inside, eyes scanning the bar for her friend, glass ready for some more bubbly, heart ready to open to whatever possibilities the evening might bring.

Theo

Theo ran a finger around his shirt collar. He rarely wore shirts, was able to dress comfortably in T-shirts and shorts or combat trousers for work. But this evening he'd been invited out for Daniel's stag party and so he'd made an effort. The damned shirt collar was driving him mad though and he couldn't wait to get home and change.

After drinks at Daniel and Willow's house, they'd made their way to The Seaside Saloon where they'd spent several hours. Then Daniel had announced that he wanted to see his fiancée and so they were headed to The White Horse where Willow's hen party was being held.

While they walked, Theo thought about how he wasn't fussy on the whole stag / hen party thing. To him it seemed old fashioned, and he couldn't imagine wanting to go through it himself, but he knew that Willow and Daniel had been encouraged to hold the traditional prewedding celebrations by their wider circle of friends. They both had friends from university and colleagues coming, as well as childhood friends, and so for them it was more of a chance to catch up with people than one to snigger at strippers and play raucous games. Not that Theo thought there was anything wrong with that sort of thing if someone liked it, more that it just wasn't his thing.

When they reached The White Horse, one of Daniel's friends made them all gather together then he asked a woman who was sitting at a table out the front of the pub to take a photo of them. Theo smiled for the camera, knowing that this was for Daniel and for Willow and that they'd no doubt add it to their shared family iCloud.

They trooped through the door to the bar and Theo scanned the room, his eyes looking for one person and one person only, because he was very aware that Chloe would be here.

He spotted Willow first, a mini veil on her head, a pink banner with *HEN* across her chest, arms in the air as she danced to a Spice Girls song. She was surrounded by other women but Theo couldn't see Chloe among them.

'Hey you.' A hand on his shoulder made him turn around and there she was.

'Chloe.' His heart squeezed as he took in how beautiful she looked in a red dress and matching heels, her blonde hair wavy, her eyes lined with grey kohl so their blue was breath taking. 'You look amazing.'

'You don't look so bad yourself.'

Her cheeks were flushed and there was a glow to her skin and Theo realised she'd had a few drinks. But so had he, although he'd been trying not to overdo it as he was past the age where a hangover in the morning was something he could get over with a coffee and a fry-up. These days, he preferred to drink in moderation and to remember the events of a night out.

'The shirt is irritating me to be honest, but I thought I should wear something other than my usual attire.'

Chloe giggled then placed a hand on his chest. 'You look fab in your T-shirts and shorts. The whole surfer vibe suits you.'

Theo swallowed hard as a memory washed over him. Chloe telling him that she couldn't see a future with him, that he wasn't who she wanted to be with, that she was tired of how content he was being a surfer, staying in the village, living his life without aspirations...

He rubbed at his chest and she withdrew her hand, her brows meeting momentarily.

'You OK?' she asked.

'Yeah. Touch of heartburn,' he lied. The last thing he wanted to do was bring the past back here tonight where it could ruin the atmosphere for his sister and brother-in-law-to-be. The last thing he wanted was to bring the past back to hurt Chloe. Seeing her again, knowing she was near... it was all he'd wanted for years and he didn't want to scare her away. The past wasn't perfect, there was pain there for sure, but he didn't want it to spoil the present or the possibilities for the future. He had no idea what Chloe wanted or needed or what she would do next, but right now, he wanted to spend time with her without dredging up what had happened over a decade ago.

Was it wrong to want to enjoy the moment without the responsibilities of the past creeping in and ruining it? If so, then he realised he was in a mood to be irresponsible.

'Drink?' He tapped her glass.

'Please.' She grinned at him then followed him to the bar, and when she slid her hand into his, he held on tight.

Willow

Willow was having a great time. Her hen night, although not a plan she'd been keen on when some of her friends first mentioned it, had turned out to be a blast. They'd sung and danced and drunk champagne and then Daniel and his stag party had arrived to round off the evening.

She looked around the bar, enjoying seeing her friends and Daniel's friends mingling, just as they would do at the wedding that was only three weeks away. She squealed inwardly at the thought, her eyes searching for Daniel then drinking him in. He really was gorgeous inside and out and she felt incredibly lucky to be marrying him. Her nan's illness had been tough but knowing that Daniel was there for her had helped; he was her rock and she could lean on him no matter what.

He caught her watching him and blew her a kiss that she returned.

And then she saw *them*.

Her brother and Chloe. Standing near the open French doors, deep in conversation.

The electricity between them was clear for anyone to see.

A lump rose in her throat. They'd both been through so much since they'd split up with Theo feeling completely lost without the woman he loved and Chloe being away from her family and friends, losing not just Theo but his family who adored her too. Willow knew that Theo and Chloe planned to pretend to be back together for Barbara's sake, but she couldn't help wondering if, on a subconscious level, there might be more to it.

As she turned back to the bar and reached for a fresh glass of champagne, she found herself hoping that there was more to it and that her brother and Chloe could have their happy ever after, after all.

Chloe

'I was outside in the garden earlier sitting on the bench.'

'The one by the tree?' Theo tilted his head as they stood in the doorway to the pub garden.

'Yes. It's still there.'

'The tree?' A smile played on his lips.

'Yes, of course the tree, but that wasn't what I meant. I was referring to the carving you did.'

'I know.'

'I didn't think it would be,' she said, thinking of their initials carved into the bark.

'Some things are forever.' His eyes seemed darker in the fading light, as if they could absorb everything, including Chloe. She could just tumble into them as if they were dark swimming pools, let go of all her fears and worries and become one with him once more. Feel safe again. Once, she'd spurned safe as boring and undesirable. Now, she knew the value of security and enduring love.

'Some things are.' She averted her gaze and sipped her drink to buy herself a moment and the bubbles tickled her nose, making her stifle a giggle.

'Let's go outside.' He took her hand and led her across the grass to the bench where they sat down.

The air was cooler than earlier and it was quiet outside, the music and chatter seeming like it was confined within the stones of the pub building, apart from the odd burst that escaped into the air. The scent of the roses was stronger now, and Chloe closed her eyes for a moment, savouring their sweetness, remembering previous evenings she'd sat here with Theo.

'How did it all go so wrong between us?' Theo's question was like a bucket of icy water over her head.

'Oh Theo...' She shook her head, not wanting to have this conversation now. Not wanting to have it ever because she'd been here before, asked herself the same thing thousands of times and while there was an answer, it also didn't seem to be enough. 'There's no simple response to that. I wish I knew exactly how to sum it all up but...' She let her sentence trail off, hoping he'd let the subject drop.

'I know what you mean.' He took her hand again, rubbed his thumb over her palm in the way he used to do. It was hypnotic, soothing, and her shoulders dropped as she sat back and sighed. 'I mean... I know that there were things that got in the way and then the more serious and devastating thing... but I loved you so much. I'd have done anything for you.'

'Except leave Sea Breeze Sands?'

Hurt widened his eyes. 'Chloe... it wasn't that straightforward. This is my home and my job's here and... my family and... everything I know.'

'I'm aware of that Theo, and I'm not blaming you. I loved you with all my heart too but I wanted to leave, to find out what life was like away from here.'

'And how is it?'

She licked her lips. 'Not that different. Lonelier. More chaotic. The same in many ways. Yet different.' She knew she was waffling. 'Reading is an amazing place but I'm on my own there. I can't afford a house and have felt there won't be much point trying to buy one anyway as I'd just rattle around in it. Plus, I don't like my job—'

'You don't?'

She laughed. 'It was never what I wanted to do. I admire teachers enormously but you know that I always wanted to write.'

'And you were brilliant at it.'

'I don't know about that.'

'You were. Your short stories were fantastic and you could still write now.'

'I don't know. I'd like to but I don't know if I can.'

'Chloe, you can do anything you put your mind to. You always could.'

There was silence as they both pondered what he'd said.

'And what about you?' she asked. 'What do you want?'

He looked down at their joined hands then his eyes rose slowly, sweeping over her to meet her gaze.

'I've always been quite simple in that respect. I don't know where we are now or what could be, but I do know that I want to enjoy spending time with you while you're back. No pressure, no expectations, just... taking it one day at a time. I'm incredibly grateful that you've agreed to act as if we're together for Nan.'

'Theo, it's no problem at all. And as for what will be...' She gave a small shrug. 'Who knows, right? My gran always says that things have a way of working out.'

Theo smiled then. 'One thing I am wondering about though is if we can appear to be convincing in our efforts to... you know... show a united front.'

'Is that right?'

Theo raised an eyebrow slowly in a way that could have seemed cocky but on him was attractive, reminding her of how he used to tease her when they were younger.

'And how do you think we can find that out?' Chloe couldn't help the smile that spread across her face, even though she knew where this was going and wasn't certain it was a good idea.

Theo placed his glass on the ground next to the bench then turned back to her and cupped her face. 'With this...' He lowered his head and pressed a soft kiss to her lips. His breath was warm and sweet from the cider he was drinking and Chloe's heart raced as he leant back slightly and met her eyes.

'That was... quite convincing,' she croaked, her throat tight with desire.

'Perhaps we'd better try again?'

'Perhaps...'

When their lips met for the second time, Chloe snaked her arms around Theo's neck and prepared to lose herself in him.

Theo

'Ahhh!' Theo pulled away from Chloe in shock and jumped up, heart racing. 'What was that?'

Looking down, he saw a wet patch spreading over his groin.

'Oh my goodness, I'm so sorry.' Chloe held up her now empty champagne glass. 'I spilt it all over you.'

Theo made a pointless attempt to brush the champagne from the material but it had already soaked in. 'I guess that might have been a good thing.'

Hurt filled Chloe's eyes. 'Oh...'

'No... I don't mean that I didn't want to kiss you... Not at all.' He sat back down and took her hand. 'All I meant was that perhaps I needed to cool down. Kissing you is incredible and maybe... I don't know... but maybe we're moving too quickly.'

'You're probably right. I mean... we are supposed to be acting. This isn't about us, it's about your nan and so we should try to remember that.'

Theo scanned her face, yearning to ask if that was how she really felt but he was held back by an old fear that still made his heart ache. After all, whatever he wanted to think or believe, Chloe had turned away from him in the past and it had cut him deeply. It could happen again and then where would he be? As much as he'd like to enjoy this and to go with it, the possibility of getting hurt meant that he probably should try to guard his heart carefully. At least until he had a better idea of exactly what it was that Chloe was feeling at this point, if she even knew herself. There was so much comfort in her touch, her proximity and in her kiss and he was enjoying it a bit too much.

Perhaps...

He stood up and held out his hand to her.

'How about I walk you home?'

She accepted his hand. 'That would be lovely.'

Hand-in-hand they went back into the pub to say their good-byes before making their way to Chloe's childhood home.

Chloe

A week later, Chloe stood in front of the full-length mirror in *Sequins and Sandals*. The dress was lovely, an ankle length navy silk affair with a fitted bodice and capped lace sleeves. The shoes she'd chosen were open toe wedges with a thin ankle strap. She felt like a little girl dressing up as a princess, something she'd done often as a child, usually with her gran's help. The two of them would raid some of the trunks filled with old clothes that her gran kept in the attic, some that had been her gran's and some that went further back to her great grandparents. Chloe wondered if her gran still had those trunks because she'd love to have a look through them now to see what else was in them. Thinking about it, they were like historical treasure troves and probably held valuable items that might well deserve a place in a clothes museum, or that could be used in period dramas on TV.

'Look at us.' Willow wrapped an arm around Chloe's shoulders and they stood gazing at their reflections. 'What a transformation.'

'We're proper grownups.'

'Very grown up, indeed.' Willow laughed. 'And we scrub up well, I think.'

'Definitely.' Chloe leant her head against Willow's and sighed. 'You look so beautiful. Daniel is a lucky man.'

'Thanks.' Willow kissed Chloe on the cheek then stepped back and ran her hands over her dress. 'I hope he likes this.'

'Of course he will. How could he not like it when you look so incredible in it?'

'I think Theo will be pretty impressed too.'

Chloe dropped her gaze to her hands and feigned interest in a jagged nail.

'Did I say the wrong thing?' Willow asked and Chloe looked up at her.

'No. Not at all. It's just... complicated.'

'I can imagine. With your history and any renewed feelings or even just a sense of nostalgia, it's probably very confusing but we all appreciate what you're doing for Nan.'

'It's no trouble.'

Chloe thought of Barbara who she'd visited every day in the past week. Sometimes, Theo had been there, but at others he'd been at work, running the family business. But he'd never been far from her mind. It was strange that after so many years of burying her thoughts about him, of pushing away her feelings, now they were bubbling to the surface too quickly for her to bat them away or to even process them. And then there was being with Theo's family, drinking cups of tea and sharing meals with them, sitting by the side of Barbara's bed and listening to her stories of her own childhood and life in Sea Breeze Sands. Barbara had been happy there for over eighty years, had fallen in love there, married and raised a family. She would die there too and had told Chloe that she was happy to do so, that she was where her heart belonged and would soon lie close to her husband, the love of her life. Chloe had coughed as sadness had surged into her throat, threatening to explode as sobs, but Barbara had taken her hand and squeezed it gently, told her that she was content to go soon. She'd followed this up by telling Chloe that she was overjoyed to have her last wish granted – having Chloe home again and reunited with Theo.

They hadn't formally announced that they were back together but had held hands in Barbara's presence, shared a hug and a chaste kiss, and so Barbara had added things up. Their plan was working, and everything was good.

Chloe could almost pretend that the past decade hadn't happened, that she was, in fact, still in a relationship with Theo and living in the village, that she'd been there all her life and all the terribly complicated and painful things hadn't happened at all. How wonderful would it be to wipe the slate clean and to forget about all that pain and heartbreak?

But, of course, life wasn't like that. There were no clean slates, no ways to expunge the past. However, there were, she knew, opportunities for new beginnings.

'Let's get out of these fancy frocks and go grab some coffee and cake, shall we?' Willow glided towards the changing cubicle, already unbuttoning the side of her dress. 'We'll be wearing them for real soon enough.'

'That's a great plan.' Chloe headed into her cubicle and pulled the curtain across. Coffee and cake was always a good idea.

Chloe

~∞~

'Don't you two look incredible.' Barbara was sitting in Lottie and Mike's lounge, dressed up in her wedding outfit of lavender trouser suit with soft white blouse and a floral fascinator.

'You look wonderful yourself, Nan,' Willow said. 'Doesn't she, Chloe?'

'Wonderful.' Chloe smiled at Barbara who dabbed at her eyes with a tissue.

The morning of the wedding had dawned and it was beautiful. Chloe had walked over after breakfast to get ready with Willow. It reminded her of when they were teens and they used to get ready together for parties and nights out, planning their outfits days in advance then sharing clothes, accessories and makeup tips as they prepared for the event ahead. Many of those times, Chloe had been getting ready to go out with Theo too, excitement fluttering in her belly like a hamster in an exercise wheel. She pressed a hand to her stomach as the full force of her feelings for him hit her. She had loved Theo deeply, had enjoyed their romance as it began like a tiny bud then flowered like a rose opening to the sun. Theo had been her first love and the only one who'd ever made a significant impression upon her heart, her life and her outlook. She'd walked away from him for reasons that made sense at the time but now... now things were different and could be different for them. Her five weeks back in Sea Breeze Sands had confirmed that for her.

At that moment, Theo appeared in the doorway. He froze and his face changed as he took in the women in their finery.

'Willow! Wow, sis. You look incredible. Just like a young Elizabeth Taylor... Wow!' He gave her a hug and she laughed.

'Thanks, Theo. Glad you think so.'

Chloe had to agree. In her pure white empire line dress with the pearl and diamanté fascinator that Rita had made for her and her long dark hair in soft ringlets that tumbled down her back, Willow made a very beautiful bride.

'Daniel's a lucky man.' His eyes strayed to Chloe and something else filled them, replacing the filial pride. 'And you look stunning, Chloe.'

'Thank you.' She felt Barbara's eyes on them and the blush that filled her cheeks grew hotter. 'I'm glad you think so.' She crossed the room and before she could chicken out, she hugged him tight then pressed a kiss to his lips. His eyes widened but then caught on and he encircled her waist with his arms, and she felt the warmth of his hands on her back. And then his mouth was on hers as he kissed her soft and slow before looking at her in a way that she could only describe as drinking her in.

'Well, well...' Barbara was chuckling now. 'At this rate there will be another wedding hot on the heels of yours, Willow.'

Chloe glanced at Willow who was nodding. 'I think you're right, Nan.'

'OK, you lot!' Mike Treharne entered the lounge carrying a tray of champagne flutes. 'Time for a toast.'

While they all accepted a glass of champagne, Lottie joined them, fresh from having her hair and makeup done in the kitchen. They'd arranged to have a makeup artist and hairstylist come to the house so all the women could have their hair and makeup done without having to go anywhere. Chloe thought they'd worked wonders on them all and she was delighted with how the hairstylist had softly waved her hair and threaded it with sprigs of gypsophila. Her makeup was neutral with a touch of sparkle on her eyelids, an uplifting silver shade blended with navy that went well with her dress.

Mike made a speech about how lucky he was to be Theo and Willow's dad as well as Lottie's husband. He thanked Barbara for being a great mother-in-law and thanked Chloe for agreeing to be Willow's bridesmaid and for bringing them all back together as a family. Chloe had to gulp down her champagne to stop the tears from falling and ruining her makeup. Mike warned them that he'd probably say similar things in his speech after the wedding ceremony but told them that he wanted to say them while they were together as a family first. He followed this with a joke about how Lottie was likely to become emotional and he didn't want her ruining her makeup, at which she swatted his arm playfully and announced to the room that it was more likely to be Mike who cried than her. The tears in his eyes as he hugged his wife showed that Lottie was right.

Glasses were refilled and Chloe perched on the sofa and listened to Theo's family as they chatted excitedly about the day ahead. Barbara was positively animated in her happiness and seemed to have regained some of the energy she'd lacked recently, the energy Chloe remembered her having.

Life was a rollercoaster with ups and downs, peaks and troughs, but this was definitely one of the ups and she was grateful to feel such simple happiness for once. There was nothing overshadowing her happy feelings today. Her oldest friend was getting married to the man she loved and Chloe would be surrounded by people she cared about. She intended on embracing the day and all the good things it would bring.

Theo

Theo pulled his phone from his pocket and glanced at the screen. It had been buzzing for a while but he'd ignored it as his parents had been speaking about Willow and Theo growing up and how proud they were of them. His nan had joined in and the champagne had flowed as they readied themselves for the day ahead.

But when he saw that the number on his phone was Daniel's, concern filled him. He really hoped things were going to plan or there would be a lot of disappointed people in Sea Breeze Sands.

'Excuse me a moment.' He held up his phone then ducked out of the lounge.

In the hallway, he accepted Daniel's call.

'OK, mate?'

'Theo...' Daniel's voice sounded thick as if he'd been coughing and hadn't cleared his throat properly.

'What's wrong?' Theo glanced at the lounge doorway and not wanting to worry Willow, he moved to the kitchen and shut the door.

On the other end of the line, Daniel sighed. 'I need to talk to you.'

'Of course. Where are you?'

'At the beach.'

'I'll come right away. But... just promise me you're OK.'

'I just need to talk, Theo.'

'Of course. On my way.'

Theo stuffed his phone back in his pocket then looked down at himself. He was already in the suit he'd bought for the wedding, a fitted navy-blue jacket, trousers and waistcoat with a white shirt and navy dress shoes. Not exactly beach gear but he didn't have time to change so he'd just have to be careful not to get anything dirty.

He popped his head into the lounge and said he had to nip back to his flat for something he'd forgotten then he left his parents' home, hoping that he'd be able to help Daniel with whatever was worrying him.

Theo hurried down to the beach, trying his best not to scuff the toes of his shoes. He was so used to wearing trainers and flipflops that dress shoes felt strange and restrictive on his feet. He had asked Willow how she'd feel about less formal footwear but her scowl had confirmed that she wouldn't want him wearing flipflops to her wedding so he'd gone in search of a pair of smart shoes.

At the seafront, he scanned the length of the beach and sure enough, perched on the top of the steps that led down to the sand, was Daniel. He sat hunched over with his head in his hands, the cliffs behind him providing a dramatic backdrop. Daniel was always such a cheerful chap with never a bad word to say about anyone so seeing him like this made unease prickle at Theo's nape.

Not wanting to waste a minute, Theo jogged along the front until he reached the steps then he descended carefully to reach Daniel's side. He sat down on the same step, taking care not to scag his trousers on the rough concrete surface.

'Daniel?'

The other man looked up and met Theo's gaze. 'You came.'

'Of course I came. You're my sister's partner but you're also my friend. Do you want to tell me what's wrong?' Dread tingled like cold sea spray on Theo's skin as he looked at Daniel. Had his sister's fiancé had a change of heart? Was he giving up on Willow on their wedding day? She would be devastated. How would Theo tell her?

'I woke up this morning and I just... I panicked. There's been so much pressure as we've prepared for the wedding. Not from Willow or our families but just from the situation. Weddings are never going to be completely stress free to plan, but I've felt the pressure building and... this morning it all got too much.'

Theo gave a brief nod to show he was listening, but he felt like he was holding his breath, afraid to say anything that might tip the scales the wrong way.

'I don't know if I can go through with it.' Daniel hung his head again and rubbed his big hands over his scalp.

Theo placed a hand on Daniel's shoulder. 'Everything will be OK.'

He swallowed. It would be wrong of him to encourage Daniel to go through with the wedding if he didn't want to. Long term, that would be a mistake for all concerned but especially for Willow. His mind went to his nan and he swallowed a groan at how upset she'd be. It might be too much for her and then she'd be sad during her final days or weeks. How could he allow this to happen to her? And yet what could he really do about it? If Daniel didn't want to get married, then it wasn't Theo's place to push him to go through with it.

Clearing his throat he said, 'Daniel... you have to do what's right for you.' He gave Daniel's back a gentle pat. 'Only get married if it's what you really want.'

Daniel turned bloodshot eyes on him. 'What if it is what I want but I don't feel...'

'You don't feel what?'

'That I'm... worthy of Willow.'

Theo almost tumbled forwards down the steps with relief. Daniel wasn't having doubts about marrying Willow because he didn't love her but was doubting himself and his own worthiness.

'You're worried that you don't deserve my sister?'

'Yes.' Daniel's eyes were so pain filled that Theo leant sideways and gave him a hug.

'You have no idea how much she loves you, do you?'

'I know she loves me now.' Daniel's Adam's apple bobbed. 'But what if that changes? What if she marries me today but there's someone better out there for her?'

'Someone better for Willow?' Theo laughed. 'There is no one better for Willow, you idiot, because you are her perfect match.'

Daniel's eyes flickered from side to side then met Theo's. 'Really?'

'I am one hundred percent certain about it. Willow loves you and has loved you since the moment she met you. I recall her telling me at the time that she'd met someone special. She was trying to stay calm and sensible and not get too excited about it but I could see it in her eyes. She loves you with her whole heart and there is no one else for her. I can't imagine there ever being someone she'd love the way she loves you.'

Daniel sat up straighter as if the information was exactly what he needed to hear.

'So marrying me is the right decision for her?'

'It's her destiny.' Theo edged on the romantic now, keen to be as encouraging as he could be.

'Her destiny. I like that.' Daniel beamed at him then looked down at himself. 'What time is it?'

Theo went to get his phone out of his pocket but Daniel had already pulled his out. 'Dammit! It's already eleven.'

'And you're not dressed.'

'No. Yikes!' Daniel stood up. 'And you're sure now?'

'I am. Willow wants to be your wife and to spend the rest of her life with you. I'm sure that some nerves the morning of your wedding are normal.'

'You won't tell her, will you? I'd hate for her to feel that I had any doubts.'

'Your doubts weren't about her, anyway, but even so, I promise I won't breathe a word of this to Willow. Just get on home and change then I'll see you at the clifftop.'

'You will. Thanks so much, Theo.'

'My pleasure.'

Theo stood up and dusted his trousers off, watching Daniel as he hurried away to get ready. Relief made Theo feel like punching the air. If Daniel had been having reservations about getting married, Theo knew it would have been natural because he was sure many people did have doubts as nerves set in. The fact that Daniel's doubts had been about whether he was good enough for Willow were ones that Theo had been able to help him to deal with. Everyone needed some reassurance now and then and he was just glad Daniel had called him.

He headed back up the steps and towards home, the sun on his face, the breeze ruffling his suit jacket. In no time at all, Willow and Daniel would be saying their vows and he was looking forward to seeing them pledging their love in front of family and friends.

Willow

Willow stood just beyond the coastal path in the area designated for the bridal party. Her family had all gone ahead to find their seats, her mum and Theo pushing her nan in a wheelchair decorated with summer flowers. Her dad was at her side, hopping from foot to foot as if he couldn't contain his excitement. Chloe was with them, looking demure in her bridesmaid dress, her bouquet of lavender and cream roses held between both hands.

Willow gazed across at the gazebo where her wedding would be held. The curtains flapped in the breeze and she could had glimpses people's backs as they waited for her arrival. This was it. She was getting married. Today, she was the bride.

She sucked in a deep breath.

Earlier on, when Theo's phone had rung and he'd dashed from the lounge of their parents' home, she'd been worried. Worried that it was Daniel having second thoughts, that everything she'd wanted, hoped and dreamt of was about to come crashing down around her ears. Because why wouldn't it? People's dreams were destroyed all the time and what made her any different? She'd been lucky so far, had a wonderful family and a loving partner, but things changed, people changed and she knew that nothing lasted forever.

What if Daniel had changed his mind? She couldn't reproach him for that although she would be devastated. Even she, loving him as deeply as she did, had experienced a few moments of hesitation over recent weeks as the wedding had grown closer. Marriage was a big deal and not to be entered into lightly. Her parents had been happily married for years but they'd had their moments of difficulty. One point had been when Chloe had left and Theo had been broken. Willow had seen the effect of the stress and worry upon her parents then, had been unable to avoid noticing how they struggled to agree on the right course of action for their son, how doubt clouded their eyes when they tried to help Theo to deal with his heartbreak. She'd sensed tension between them and overheard a few heated exchanges between them when they thought no one was nearby. But they had got through it, they had been there for Theo in every way possible and he had grown stronger again and found his own kind of peace. Willow loved her brother and had done what she could for him too, but Theo being the man he was had put on a brave face and soldiered on. He'd smiled, lifted his chin and appeared to be coping but Willow had seen the occasional flashes of pain in his eyes, the way his smile dropped when he thought no one was looking. She knew their nan had been brilliant with him, managing to make him laugh and offering pearls of wisdom when he needed it most, and so they had got through that time together as a family. Willow knew her family would have done the same for her had the situation been different and that Theo would have been there to hold her up, her biggest supporter. He had grown into a good man with a big heart.

Her eyes moved from the gazebo to Chloe. She hoped Chloe did still care for Theo as deeply as it seemed. If Chloe and Theo could be reunited, then Willow would have everything she could wish for. The love Theo and Chloe felt for each other was evident in the way they gazed at each other, but they had some things to overcome first, before they could be together properly. Only time would tell if they were meant to be.

Her dad's mobile pinged and he checked the screen then looked at Willow.

'Are you ready, angel?'

She inclined her head and her heart fluttered like a tiny bird against her ribcage.

'I'm ready, Dad.'

Chloe gave Willow a quick hug. 'Thank you for asking me to be your bridesmaid. I'm so happy to be here for your special day.'

'I'm delighted you're here. I wouldn't have it any other way.' Willow kissed Chloe's cheek then she accepted her dad's arm while Chloe went to stand a few paces in front of them.

Slowly, they walked across the grass towards the gazebo while the acoustic band hired for the day played the opening notes of John Legend's *All of Me*. The curtains of the gazebo were opened wide by the ushers and Chloe made her way along the aisle towards the small platform at the other end of the gazebo that overlooked the beach. The guests oohed and aahed as Chloe passed them in her beautiful dress. Willow spotted Theo at the front near Daniel, his eyes fixed on Chloe as if he were the groom and she the bride.

One day, perhaps...

And when Chloe took her place at the side of the platform, all heads turned slowly to Willow and her dad. He gave her hand a squeeze then they began the walk towards her future.

Willow fixed her eyes on Daniel, admiring how handsome he was in his bright white shirt, bow tie, navy suit and waistcoat. He didn't seem to blink as she approached him, emotion filling his gaze. He seemed unsure what to do with his hands, as if they were the part of him revealing his inner emotions by twisting around each other, heading to his pockets then back out again. It made her want to reach him quickly so she could take his hands in hers and reassure him that everything would be just fine.

And then, they'd arrived at the front. Chloe took Willow's bouquet, a larger version of Chloe's one with cream roses and lavender, and Willow's dad hugged her and whispered, 'I'm so proud of you and I love you very much.'

'Love you too, Dad.'

She turned back to Daniel.

'Hello.' Daniel took Willow's hands. 'You look incredibly beautiful.'

'What? In this old thing.' She giggled.

'You're the most beautiful woman I've ever seen and I love you with all of my heart.'

'And I love you.'

Daniel leant forwards and kissed her and the registrar, a tall man called Toby, with pink dreadlocks and a white goatee beard, cleared his throat loudly. 'Excuse me. The kiss is meant to come after I pronounce you married.'

Everyone laughed and there were a few wolf whistles.

Toby grinned. 'Are we ready to begin?'

'I am,' Willow said.

'Me too.' Daniel nodded.

'Wonderful!' Toby bobbed his head. 'Today we are gathered here to celebrate the wedding of this lovely couple...'

Chloe

~~~

'And now you may kiss the bride,' Toby said with a big grin, revealing teeth capped with gold. She knew he was a friend of Theo's who he'd met through surfing and couldn't imagine a nicer man to conduct the ceremony.

As Willow and Daniel kissed, the guests cheered and clapped, and Chloe had to bite down hard on her bottom lip to stop herself bursting into tears. Everything had been perfect and exactly how she'd once dreamt her own wedding might go.

Looking up, she met Theo's gaze. He was clapping hard but his eyes were on Chloe, not the newly married couple. She blinked, stirred by the intensity of his gaze, wondering how to conduct herself in front of so many people. Then Theo flashed her a smile and warmth flooded through her. At his side, Barbara was smiling too, and when Theo turned to her, she held out a hand so he could help her to her feet. With his arm supporting her, she clapped and cheered, and it was such an emotional moment that Chloe felt like her heart burst.

When the newlyweds finally stopped kissing, the band started to play again and Journey's *Don't Stop Believin* filled the air. Chloe handed Willow her bouquet then she walked along the aisle with her new husband as guests threw dried flower confetti over them and the official photographer snapped away with her hi-tech digital camera.

When Willow and Daniel had left the gazebo, Chloe turned and gazed out at the clifftop. From there she could see across to the other side of the beach where cliffs hugged the bay and the clifftop housing development – where Willow and Daniel lived – sat in a prime position. The sky was flawless blue, the breeze warm and gentle and the sea glinted in the sunlight as if it had been filled with hundreds of thousands of diamonds.

The ceremony, the couple and the location were all perfect and Chloe's heart was filled with joy that she was home to see it all.

Theo

The ceremony had been wonderful and now the reception was well underway. Willow and Daniel had arranged to hold it at the village hall so the wedding party walked back there, enjoying the beautiful weather.

Theo had pushed his nan's wheelchair and she'd chatted happily all the way back. Chloe had joined them, along with her mum and gran and it had felt like old times to have them all together again. Nora Nancarrow entertained them with stories about her own wedding and about people she and Theo's nan had known who were long gone. In some ways, it felt sad talking about those who were no longer alive but in others, it was positive because it made Theo realise that no one was every truly gone. There would always be someone to remember them, to hold memories of them dear, whether close or distant family member, friend or acquaintance. Nora had also known Theo's grandad quite well and his nan loved talking about her husband, so they regaled them with funny stories about what a character Bill Rees had been.

Of course, Theo could remember his grandpa, as Bill had only passed away ten years ago, but he'd known Bill as an elderly man and not as the young man Barbara and Nora had. Apparently, Bill had loved to swim and had spent a great deal of his time in the water, sometimes to his wife's frustration because she worried when he went swimming in inclement weather. One day, he'd been gone for hours, far longer than expected, and Barbara had sent the coastguard out looking for him. They'd found him around the coast on an isolated beach, wearing swimming trunks with a borrowed blanket wrapped around his shoulders, eating sandwiches with a family holidaying in the area. He'd been tired and his blood sugar low after a long swim so when he'd washed up on the beach the family had offered him some of their picnic.

Bill had been a jovial man according to all accounts and able to charm anyone into friendship. Theo couldn't help thinking that he was quite different from his grandpa, far quieter and more reserved. He wasn't a fan of large crowds or speaking to people he didn't know well. However, like his grandpa, Theo felt most comfortable in the sea, when he was alone with the waves and his surfboard.

In the village hall, Theo was sitting at one of the round tables next to his nan and he leant forwards and touched her arm.

'Can I get you anything, Nan?'

She pursed her lips and wrinkled her brow. 'A glass of lemonade would be lovely, thank you.'

He nodded then got up and went to the bar where he ordered a lemonade and a bottle of beer. Leaning against the bar, he looked around the hall. There were ten of the large round tables with white tablecloths, rose, lavender and driftwood centrepieces and lavender sashes looped around the chairs. Willow and Daniel hadn't wanted a traditional top table because they wanted their friends and family to mingle around them and so they sat at a round table in the centre of the hall. At the one end of the hall was a stage and on there, a DJ had set up and was currently playing a range of love songs. In front of the stage was a space set up as a dancefloor where some couples were already slow dancing.

Chloe was at a table with her mum and gran as well as some

of Willow and Daniel's friends. She was talking to a woman on her right, nodding and smiling, her beautiful face lighting up the room.

The song ended and Ellie Goulding's version of *Your Song* came on. A wave of memories hit Theo just as Chloe locked up and locked eyes with him.

He knew instantly what he had to do.

He took the drinks to the table and handed his nan her lemonade then he hurried over to Chloe. He held out a hand and when she accepted it, he led her to the dancefloor.

They gazed at each other for a moment then he took her in his arms, one hand holding hers, the other in the centre of her back. They moved slowly, eyes locked, both remembering the first time they'd heard the song, the first time they'd danced to it at a friend's engagement party. Back then Theo had no idea what was coming or how their lives would change, he'd believed that he'd be with Chloe always and forever. For years, that had seemed an impossibility but now, as she rested her head against his chest, he wondered if there was a chance that this could be the start of the life he'd once dreamt of having.

Chloe

~∂∂つ~

When the song ended, Chloe stayed where she was for a moment, trying to catch her breath. She'd been happy to accept Theo's hand then follow him to the dance floor and dancing with Theo had brought back lovely memories. As they'd danced, everything else had faded away and it had felt like it was just her and Theo, alone at last.

Looking into his eyes now, she knew that her feelings for him hadn't died, that they'd been tucked away in her heart, locked away in a box at the back of her mind so she could cope. Had she allowed her love for Theo to burn brightly then daily life would have been impossible. She'd have pined for him, longed to be with him and she'd needed to not feel those things so she could work and function as a human being. But back in Sea Breeze Sands, it was impossible to deny how she felt about Theo.

The question now was what they were going to do about it. Theo's eyes conveyed the same confusing maelstrom of thoughts and feelings that she was experiencing, and she wished she could take it all away for him and simply make him happy again. Why did human beings find it so difficult to be happy sometimes? Why had Chloe striven to find a different life when it seemed clear that what she'd wanted and needed was right here all along?

'Drink?' Theo asked, glancing around them at the guests who were bobbing to an upbeat song.

'Please.'

They went to the bar where Chloe ordered a glass of champagne.

'Are you having one?'

'I have a beer already at the table. Do you want to come and sit with me?'

Just then there was a tinkling as Mike Treharne tapped a spoon on the side of his glass.

'Looks like it's time for the speeches so I'd better go back to my table,' she said even though it wasn't what she wanted to do. 'I'll join you afterwards.'

She squeezed Theo's hand and went to walk away but he hadn't let go of her, so she jolted backwards.

His gaze burned into her then he lowered his head and pressed a kiss to her lips before releasing her hand. She floated to her table and sat down, pressing a hand to her lips that still tingled, a powerful reminder of what Theo could do to her with a simple kiss.

The speeches were beautiful. Mike's was very similar to the one he'd made that morning with a few extra mentions, Daniel's was sweet and funny and Willow made a witty and moving speech. When she ended with special thanks to her nan, Chloe had to bury her face in her napkin. It was such a bittersweet day, wonderful in many ways but knowing that Barbara didn't have long left was heartbreaking. Chloe knew that she'd have hated herself if she hadn't come back and spent this time with Barbara and her family.

As the light waned and the evening celebrations got underway, bringing more guests, a lavish buffet of locally sourced foods and more dancing, Chloe excused herself and went outside to get some air.

'Chloe?'

She turned from gazing at the burnished-gold sky to find Theo in the doorway.

'Everything all right?'

'I'm just a bit tired.' She yawned and stretched her arms. 'It's been fabulous but I was up early and it's been busy.'

'And emotional.' He came to her side. 'I'm quite worn out myself.'

'How's Barbara?'

'She's tired too. I said I'll take her home soon.'

'Will you come back?'

'I don't think so. There are a lot of people in there now and while it's my sister's wedding and I feel I should be there, I also think someone should be with Nan. It's not fair for my parents to leave the party so I'll take her home and stay with her.'

Chloe knew that Theo would want to be there for his nan if she needed him. Time was short and he wanted to treasure every moment.

'Would you... like some company?'

'You don't want to stay here and dance the night away?'

Chloe licked her lips. Pushed her hair behind her ears. Sighed. 'Not without you.'

Meeting Theo's gaze, she knew she'd said the right thing.

'I'll go and take Nan around to say her goodbyes then I'll grab a bottle of champagne and we can have it at home. Well... at my parents' home.' He grinned.

'Sounds good to me.'

She watched as Theo went back inside, taking a moment to steady herself, then she went after him, keen to say her own goodbyes so she could head home with him and Barbara. She could already taste the crisp champagne and smell the honeysuckle and roses of his parents' garden, could anticipate the feel of Theo's hand in hers and the soft caress of his lips as he kissed her under the Sea Breeze Sky.

Chloe

Theo pulled Barbara's bedroom door behind him but left it open a crack.

'She OK?' Chloe asked.

'Wiped out and I'm not surprised.' Theo yawned and Chloe did too, the chain reaction making her smile.

'You're tired too.'

'But I'd like to sit in the garden and share that champagne with you. And...' He waggled his eyebrows. 'I don't know about you but I'm hungry too.'

Chloe laughed. 'The fancy dinner didn't fill you up?'

'It did at the time but then I missed the buffet because the line was so long and I wanted to get Nan home.'

'I'm sure there's something in the fridge or freezer.' Chloe knew that Theo's parents always kept the fridge and freezer well stocked.

Theo opened the fridge door and leaned into it then emerged with a shake of his head. He opened the freezer instead and pulled out a pizza box. 'Three cheese special?'

'Yum!'

Once the pizza was in the oven, Theo opened the champagne then they went outside and sat at the table. He lit the citronella candle at the centre and Chloe watched as the flame flickered, casting shadows across the wooden surface.

'What a day,' he said, picking up his glass.

'It was brilliant. Willow and Daniel looked so happy.'

'They are and they'll have an amazing life together.'

'I hope so.'

'And what about you, Chloe? What's your plan now?' He looked down at his glass and ran a finger through the condensation on the side.

'My plan?'

'Yes... Are you heading back to Reading soon or...'

He let his sentence trail off and Chloe felt the tension building in the air between them.

'I... I'm not sure anymore. It's so good to be home. And... there's Barbara to think of, and...'

'You'll stay for Nan?'

Chloe gazed at him through the gathering dusk. His eyes were so dark, so intense, so beautiful.

'I don't want to leave before...' She bit her tongue. Was she about to say before Barbara passed away? It sounded so awful.

'It's OK, I understand.' He drained his glass. 'But what—'

'About you?'

'I was going to say *us*.'

'Oh Theo... I'm not sure. It's been incredible spending time with you again but every time I try to think ahead, to work out where this is going... it's hard because so many other people are affected by what we do.'

'I know. I know.' He hung his head and Chloe felt like her heart would break. She couldn't do this to him now, couldn't see him sad when he had so much to deal with. She did care for him, did have deeper feelings for him but what she should do with those feelings was confusing. They could get back together, could make this work, could find a way if they wanted to. If they really wanted to.

But right now, Chloe just wanted to be close to this man and to make him feel good.

She put her glass on the table then got up and went to him. Standing in front of him, still wearing her bridesmaid's dress, she was conscious of the silk against her skin, the cool evening air, the goosebumps rising on her arms even though she wasn't cold.

Theo raised his hands and rested them on her hips then began to lift her dress slowly up her legs until it was bunched up in his hands. She stepped closer and moved onto his lap, straddling him, then he pulled her closer and kissed her.

At first his kiss was soft, featherlight, then it deepened and Chloe wrapped herself around him, losing herself in the pleasure of the moment and in the joy of holding him once more. Some things might be confusing, but being with Theo in this way was the perfect way to end a beautiful day.

Theo

Waking the next morning, Theo experienced a surge of joy. Had last night really happened? After the wedding, he'd gone back to his parent's home with his nan and Chloe. He'd settled his nan in bed then gone out to the garden with Chloe and they'd shared a bottle of champagne. They'd talked for a bit then ended up kissing. The kissing had led to more and they'd made love right there in the garden, the stars twinkling above them, the cool evening air washing over their skin, the pizza still cooking in the oven.

When his parents got home, tipsy and tired after a busy day, Theo and Chloe had left. He'd expected to walk her home but instead, she'd come back to his flat above the shop. They'd fallen into bed together, exhausted and sated, only stirring in the early hours to make love again.

He turned over now, expecting to find Chloe lying next to him but she was gone. He placed a hand on the side of the bed where she'd slept and it was cool, the sheets ruffled, the pillow bearing an indent from her head. He shuffled over to the pillow and buried his face in it, inhaling Chloe's scent, trying to hold on to the night for just a few more moments.

Perhaps last night had been foolish. Surrendering to desire and yearning for another person would always be risky, but when it was with the person he'd loved with his whole heart, it was a huge risk to take. And yet, Theo had no regrets. Over the years, he'd wondered if the love he'd felt for Chloe had been real, as tangible as it had felt at the time, and now he knew. Chloe was a wonderful human being and even though he'd tried to get over her, now he knew he never would.

His mobile buzzed on the bedside table so he reached for it and squinted at the screen. Heart lurching as he read the message asking him to call home, he sat up against the pillows and sucked in a deep breath to steel himself before unlocking the screen and scrolling to his dad's number.

Chloe

'What time did you roll in?'

Chloe peered at her gran over her mug of black coffee and shrugged. Her gran looked fresh faced and bright eyed and was wearing a pair of beige linen trousers and floaty white blouse. Behind her glasses, her grey eyes danced with mischief.

'I was up at sunrise doing yoga and I don't think you were back then.' Her gran twisted her mouth. 'So I'm guessing you stayed out all night.'

'Please stop it.' Chloe rubbed her eyes then hunched back over the table.

'Oh Chloe, I'm sorry, I was only teasing. Are you all right?'

Her gran crossed the kitchen and placed a hand on Chloe's shoulder. Chloe swallowed hard.

'I... I'm not sure. I feel very mixed up this morning.' Chloe placed a hand over her gran's. 'I didn't mean to be rude.'

'I know that, my sweetheart. Now... what can I do to help?'

Her gran sat down and Chloe sagged against her. 'I think I did something stupid last night.'

'Why's that?'

'I spent the night with Theo.' Her cheeks grew hot.

'And you feel it was a mistake?'

'I'm not sure.'

'Did you want to spend the night with him?'

Chloe nodded.

'Well there you go then. As long as it was something you both wanted then it wasn't a mistake.'

'But there are things we still haven't discussed. Things we didn't work through before and it's like we've both been pretending that those things don't exist.'

Her gran rubbed her shoulder. 'What about if you do talk to him? Tell him how you're feeling and see what he says. I'm sure Theo wants to clear the air too.'

Chloe sat back and sipped her coffee. The kitchen was warm with morning sunlight, the floor golden where the rays fell across it. The sky beyond the window was bright blue without a cloud in sight.

'It's your life, Chloe, and you have to live it the way you want. But don't let pride or fear stop you from going after whatever it is that you really want. People make mistakes and do things they wish they hadn't but the human capacity for forgiveness and healing is incredible. If you feel that you and Theo have something worth saving, then you need to address any issues head on and deal with them. You get one life, my precious girl, and it passes in the blink of an eye so please don't waste time worrying.'

Chloe put her mug down and snuggled into her gran, breathing in her violet scent, and enjoying the security that came from hugging this wonderful woman who had been there for her all her life, who always had words of wisdom and time and love to spare.

'Thank you, Gran.'

'Whatever for?'

'Being you.'

Her gran squeezed her tight and Chloe closed her eyes, savouring the moment.

When her mobile buzzed on the table, she ignored it but when it buzzed repeatedly, her gran leant forwards and picked it up. 'I think you need to see this, Chloe,' she said, passing the phone to her.

Glancing at the screen, Chloe's stomach dropped to the floor and she gasped.

'Oh goodness... oh no.' She stood up. 'I need to go to him.'

Her gran nodded, a grave smile on her face. 'He needs you now.'

'Yes.' Chloe gave her gran a quick hug then she went to the hallway and pushed her feet into her trainers and grabbed her cardigan from the hook.

She had left Theo that morning because she felt she needed space after spending the night with him but now everything had changed and all she could think was that she had to be there for him.

Right now...

Chloe

The service had been beautiful. Moving. Uplifting. A celebration of Barbara's life. It had been held on the clifftop in the same spot where Willow and Daniel had married less than two weeks ago. Chloe had been at Theo's side, holding his hand, dabbing at her eyes as Lottie spoke about her mum and what a wonderful person she'd been.

Barbara had slipped away the morning after the wedding. She'd stirred when Lottie and Mike had got home and gone in to check on her, smiled, and told them she'd had the most marvellous day. Lottie had sat with her mum until she'd dropped back off to sleep then headed up to bed. The next morning, it had been around six when Lottie had gone down to make tea. She'd popped her head around Barbara's bedroom door and known immediately that something was different.

And though they were all incredibly sad that Barbara had gone, there was comfort to be found in her peaceful passing and in knowing that her pain was over. Throughout the wedding and the party afterwards, Barbara had smiled and laughed, had even enjoyed some champagne, and then she'd passed quietly in her sleep. Chloe couldn't think of a better way to go and Theo, though devastated, had agreed.

Barbara's body was to be buried with her husband's in the village cemetery so the family would soon make their way down there along with the funeral director, then the wake was being held at the village hall.

They said their goodbyes to the other mourners then walked down to the village, Chloe, Theo and his family, her gran and mum. As they walked, they shared their memories of Barbara and funny things she'd said over the years. Chloe felt a deep sadness in her heart, but it was balanced out by love and hope. Barbara had gone but she would live on through them all, afforded eternal life through how much she was loved.

Later that day, Chloe sighed as the cool seawater washed over her feet. It had been a long day and she was emotionally drained, but she was doing her best to stay strong for Theo because she could see how much he was struggling.

They had left the wake before the rest of his family. Theo had asked Chloe to go down to the beach with him and she'd agreed, liking the idea of a walk and some quiet time after being with so many people throughout the day. It had seemed that the whole village had come out to show their respect for Barbara and the repeated shaking of hands had been tiring for Theo, the acceptance of condolences draining. But he had held himself together, had even raised a toast to his nan at the wake, his words so sweet that Chloe had almost crumbled.

They stood now with their feet in the water. Theo had removed his jacket and rolled up his shirt sleeves and trouser legs. His face was bathed in the peachy late afternoon light, his eyes seeming luminous as they gazed out to sea.

Finally, he turned to Chloe and took her hand. 'We need to talk.'

She swallowed. 'What? Now?'

'I can't wait any longer. I need to understand.'

'During the two weeks since Barbara's passing, they hadn't broached other serious subjects, had focused on planning the funeral and dealing with their grief. Chloe had stayed with Theo every night, holding him tight while fat tears fell silently onto his pillow. She had been there for him as he needed her to be and she'd known that when he was ready, they would talk properly. But today? Was it the right time when they were so tired and emotional? Shouldn't they wait?

As if reading her thoughts, he shook his head. 'I need to do it now. I need to know why you left and what you want going forwards. Please, Chloe, be honest with me because I don't want false hope if there's none to be found.'

He raised a hand and stroked her cheek, his eyes filled with painful emotions she couldn't bear to see.

'OK.' She sighed. 'Let's go and sit down and then we can talk.'

They made their way up the beach to the sand dunes where they sat down, side by side, facing the sea and the rose-gold horizon.

Theo was right. The time for transparency had arrived, however hard it might be to share exactly what was on her mind, whatever the outcome of being completely honest might be.

Theo

Theo felt like he could lie down on the sand and sleep but he couldn't give way to the tiredness, not yet. He'd been blinkered the past few days, his attention focused on getting through his nan's funeral, on being there for his mum and dad, on being strong for his family. He knew that while he'd been trying to hold it together, Chloe had been there for him, his quiet rock, a hand ready to steady him every time the ground swayed beneath his feet. And it had swayed, several times, but Chloe had been there and he had clung to her.

However, he'd known that the time would come when he'd have to face up to reality and to the fact that Chloe might not be sticking around. Being with her again had been wonderful, magical, even with such sad circumstances, but if she needed to go then he had to support that. Sometimes loving someone meant letting them go. Chloe deserved to live the life she wanted and if he had to wave goodbye to her again then he would do it with a smile on his face even if his heart was fracturing.

Chloe sighed deeply then she hugged her knees to her chest and rested her chin on them. 'Theo... being here in Sea Breeze Sands again has been eye-opening. I've loved spending time with you and your family, am so grateful to Willow for inviting me to be her bridesmaid and to your family for welcoming me back with open arms. Your nan...' Her voice wavered so she swallowed hard. 'Barbara... she was such an amazing person and I'm so glad I got to spend time with her before...' She wiped at her eyes then wrapped her arms back around her legs. 'I wouldn't have missed these past weeks for anything. Being with you... what a gift that has been.' She turned her head to face him and he saw the tears in her beautiful eyes, the pain etched on her features.

This was hard for her. He braced himself.

'We were so young when we got together and I loved you fiercely. You were all I could think about for so long but we had lives ahead of us and I'd always wanted to go to university and was happy when I got a place on the course. As you know, I also wanted to live in a city at some point and back then it all seemed so important.' She shook her head. 'But things change. City life has lots going for it but as I've got older, it's lost some of the appeal.'

'That's a shame,' he said, wanted to show that he cared about the fact that her dream of city life had been rocked.

'It's OK and it's certainly not your fault. I did what I needed to do and moving to Reading was the right thing for me at that time.'

'I'm happy you did it because if you hadn't, you'd always have wondered if there was something better.'

Chloe knitted her brows. 'Yes. I think that's true. And that was where we differed. When I was in my late teens and early twenties, the fact that we wanted different things like that seemed like the end of the world. I wanted you to see things my way and—'

'I did try.'

She rubbed at her forehead. 'You did. I know that but it didn't change our differing feelings about living here on the coast and living in a city. I worried that we couldn't make things work when we had such different ideas about lifestyle. And then it all changed anyway when I got... pregnant.'

Theo gulped. Hearing the words was so hard even after such a long time. He tried not to think too often of the baby they made, the tiny being that didn't make it, but it crept in sometimes, haunting dreams that he woke from with tears on his cheeks. Until then he'd had no idea that a person could care for something that hadn't been born, that didn't have life outside of its mother's womb.

'Finding out I was pregnant in my third year of university when I went back to Reading after Christmas was just terrifying. I'd already started to have doubts about us and what would become of our relationship because we seemed to want such different things and suddenly, we were having a child. I hadn't even finished my degree course and we had another human being to consider. When I came home, by that point eleven weeks pregnant, and told you... I wasn't sure what you'd say but you were elated.'

'Of course I was. I loved you and couldn't see how it would be a problem for us.'

'Oh Theo...' She reached over and took his hand, lacing her fingers through his. 'I wanted it to be that simple but I also wanted to finish my degree. My mother got pregnant with me and gave up everything to be a mum and I was wary of repeating that. She surrendered all of her dreams to care for me and I didn't know if I could do the same thing. She was so selfless, but I worried I'd resent a baby if it stopped me studying for my MA in Creative Writing.'

'I never wanted you to give all that up. I just thought perhaps you could postpone it until after the baby was born.'

'In retrospect, I can see that but at the time I was so emotional and convinced that I should be career orientated, that I couldn't become like my mother. She's an incredible woman and she's done well. She's created a whole career in art for herself that didn't require travelling the world like she'd planned on doing before she got pregnant with me. But I do wonder if she has any regrets. Sometimes, I think she must. She loved my dad deeply and was happy with him but losing him as she did left her without any security and I was terrified of ending up in the same situation.'

Theo nodded. He knew Chloe's mum had struggled after she lost her husband because she had built her whole life around him and Chloe. He'd also known that Chloe feared ending up like her mum because she'd told him so when they first got together, and he'd understood that fear.

'And then we argued.' Chloe grimaced. 'Such a horrible, painful argument.'

'I know and I'm so sorry. I was just worried about you and the baby. Then there was the party. That stupid party.' He winced with pain as the memory pierced his mind.

'Seeing you with the girl all over you like that... it boiled my blood.'

'She meant nothing, and I did push her away but... you walked in at the wrong moment. I never wanted anyone other than you.'

'She had her arms draped around your neck and she was trying to kiss you and it made me feel sick to my stomach. I had to get out of there.'

'I wish I could take it all back and go and change what happened that night.'

'Me too. But after I shouted at you both and ran off... I convinced myself that it was a sign that I should leave the village.'

'Did I cause the miscarriage, Chloe?' Theo's voice shook. 'That's what I've been afraid of. That I was responsible for us losing our baby.'

'No.' She shook her head, tears in her eyes. 'It wasn't you and it wasn't me. For a long time, I blamed myself and at times I blamed you, but it was just one of those things. The doctor who treated me at the hospital told me that the pregnancy wasn't viable and the baby wouldn't have made it. A lot of first pregnancies end in miscarriage.'

'It was awful. I hated myself for hurting you.'

'I felt the same about hurting you. But it was just the wrong time. Life can be cruel.'

They sat in silence for a while, absorbing everything that had been said. The waves lapped at the shore as the tide came in and swallows swooped and soared like hundreds of small black marks slashed upon the horizon.

'Deciding to abandon my dream of doing a creative writing course was a way of punishing myself. I was angry with myself for hurting you and I felt like a failure for losing the baby. I hadn't wanted to be pregnant and I felt responsible for losing the baby, as if I'd somehow brought the miscarriage on. I needed to decide on a career path and a PGCE seemed like a good option.'

Theo smiled in spite of the seriousness of their conversation. 'I'd always imagined you being a writer and never once thought you'd go into teaching.'

'Nor me. There have been good things about the job but I have to admit that my heart's not in it.'

'So what will you do now?'

'I think the time has come for us to both forgive ourselves. Not just paying it lip service but really accepting that the miscarriage wasn't our fault and letting go of the sadness. We have to let go before we can move on.'

'But Chloe... do you forgive me?'

'Theo, there's nothing to forgive. We were young and we made some choices back then that we probably wouldn't make now.'

'That's true. I'd be far more sensitive to what you want.'

'You always were sensitive and thoughtful, Theo, but the pregnancy was a shock and you wanted to do the right thing. I'm sure that if it had worked out differently, we'd have found a way to be parents. I suspect we'd have stayed together too. Not just for the child but because... we loved each other.'

'I still love you, Chloe.' He squeezed her hand, unable to do anything other than be completely honest with her. 'I always have.'

She smiled sadly, lowering her gaze to their joined hands and Theo held his breath, bracing himself for the moment when she'd tell him she cared for him but was leaving.

'Theo… during my time here I've come to realise things that were not previously clear to me. And the most important thing of all is that I do love you, with all my heart. I always have done and always will do.'

He sucked in a breath. 'Enough to want to stay?'

Chloe smiled and relief flooded through him. 'More than enough. I've missed you, the village, your family and mine. I was running away from a life I thought I didn't want but now I can't imagine wanting any other kind of life.'

Theo punched the air with his free hand and Chloe laughed.

'Theo… can we try again?'

'A thousand times, yes.' He pulled her closer then kissed her, sending out thanks to the universe for bringing the woman he loved home at last.

Epilogue - Chloe

Chloe stood gazing out at the goose-grey horizon, shivering as the winter wind whipped around her legs and crept underneath her hat. November had come to Sea Breeze Sands bringing bitter winds and icy mornings. But however cold she might get on the outside, inside she glowed with happiness.

She'd moved back to the village in the summer, giving notice to the supply agency and to her landlord. Initially, she'd stayed with her mum and gran, wanting to get to know Theo better again before committing to living with him. But they'd spent every night and all their free time together, so when he'd asked her to move into the flat with him, it had seemed like a sensible step.

She'd started to write again, had taken several online courses and was enjoying herself. She helped Theo out in the surf shop a few days a week as well as helping at her gran's shop too, and she was enjoying the more relaxed pace of life, especially in light of her condition.

Placing a hand on her rounded belly, she smiled.

'Everything OK?' Theo wrapped an arm around her shoulders.

'Absolutely fine.'

'I just worry when I see you touch your stomach... you know... in case...'

'Nothing's wrong.' She leant her head on him. 'I'm just happy.'

Since finding out she was pregnant, Theo had been jittery as a cat on a hot tin roof. She was around sixteen weeks along now, which meant that the baby had been conceived the night of Willow and Daniel's wedding. Secretly, Chloe thought that it seemed appropriate. The night that Barbara had left the world, Chloe and Theo had conceived their child. When one human being left their body, another came into existence. It was almost like Barbara had willed it so.

Their early scans had come back clear and the pregnancy was strong. They were, to their joy, expecting a girl, and they'd decided that Barbara would be the baby's middle name. Theo was delighted and called the baby 'Little B' whenever he spoke to Chloe's bump. He would be a wonderful father, Chloe knew, and she was excited about their life together.

'I've been thinking...' Theo rubbed at the back of his neck.

'Oh, don't do that. It's dangerous.' Chloe chuckled and Theo smiled but a muscle in his jaw twitched. 'I... uh... I...'

'What is it, my love?' She turned to him and cupped his face in her gloved hands.

'Well... in her will... Nan left me something and I've been carrying it around in my pocket waiting for the right time to ask you something.'

Chloe's heart jumped and her mouth fell open. Was he going to ask her what she thought he might?

Theo gently removed her left glove then kissed her hand. 'I love you so much and I want to devote the rest of my life to you and Little B. Chloe... I swear to spend every day caring for you and doing what I can to make you and our baby happy. Nan left me this and I think I know why she did.' He slid a hand into his coat pocket and brought out a rose gold ring with a sapphire at the centre nestled between two diamonds.

Chloe's vision blurred. 'It's Barbara's engagement ring.'

'Yes. Chloe...' He dropped to one knee and held out the ring. 'Will you marry me?'

She stared at the ring, the stones seeming to sparkle with something magical. Inside her stomach there was a fluttering and she placed her free hand there to connect with the baby. Their child had given her a sign that this was the right thing to do, even though she had no doubt in her mind that this was exactly what she wanted.

'Theo... I love you with all my heart and would be honoured to share my life with you.'

Theo slid the ring on her finger then stood up and kissed her. Being in his arms was where she was always meant to be, she thought, it just took her a while to work it out.

She held up her left hand and admired the ring, a symbol of eternal love, and she felt that love encircling her as protectively as Theo's arms. Coming home to Sea Breeze Sands had brought Chloe back to where she belonged and all because of her best friend's wedding.

Soon, they would have a wedding of their own.

The End...

Dear Reader,

Thank you so much for reading *THE WEDDING*. I hope you enjoyed reading it as much as I enjoyed writing it.

Did the story make you smile, laugh or even cry? Did you care about the characters?

If you can spare five minutes of your time, I would be so grateful if you could leave a rating and a short review.

Stay safe and well!

With love,

Rachel X

Acknowledgments

Firstly, thanks to my gorgeous family. I love you so much!

To my friends, for your support, advice and encouragement, huge heartfelt thanks!

To everyone who buys, reads and reviews this book, thank you.

About the Author

Rachel Griffiths is an author, wife, mother, Earl Grey tea drinker, gin enthusiast, dog walker and fan of the afternoon nap. She loves to read, write and spend time with her family.

What To Read Next...

CWTCH COVE SERIES
CHRISTMAS AT CWTCH COVE
WINTER WISHES AT CWTCH COVE
MISTLETOE KISSES AT CWTCH COVE
THE COTTAGE AT CWTCH COVE
THE CAFÉ AT CWTCH COVE
CAKE AND CONFETTI AT CWTCH COVE
A NEW ARRIVAL AT CWTCH COVE

THE COSY COTTAGE CAFÉ SERIES
SUMMER AT THE COSY COTTAGE CAFÉ
AUTUMN AT THE COSY COTTAGE CAFÉ
WINTER AT THE COSY COTTAGE CAFÉ
SPRING AT THE COSY COTTAGE CAFÉ
A WEDDING AT THE COSY COTTAGE CAFÉ
A YEAR AT THE COSY COTTAGE CAFÉ (THE
COMPLETE SERIES)

THE LITTLE CORNISH GIFT SHOP SERIES
CHRISTMAS AT THE LITTLE CORNISH GIFT SHOP
SPRING AT THE LITTLE CORNISH GIFT SHOP

SUMMER AT THE LITTLE CORNISH GIFT SHOP
THE LITTLE CORNISH GIFT SHOP (THE COMPLETE SERIES)

SUNFLOWER STREET SERIES
SPRING SHOOTS ON SUNFLOWER STREET
SUMMER DAYS ON SUNFLOWER STREET
AUTUMN SPICE ON SUNFLOWER STREET
CHRISTMAS WISHES ON SUNFLOWER STREET
A WEDDING ON SUNFLOWER STREET
A NEW BABY ON SUNFLOWER STREET
NEW BEGINNINGS ON SUNFLOWER STREET
SNOWFLAKES AND CHRISTMAS CAKES ON SUNFLOWER STREET
A YEAR ON SUNFLOWER STREET (SUNFLOWER STREET BOOKS 1-4)
THE COSY COTTAGE ON SUNFLOWER STREET
SNOWED IN ON SUNFLOWER STREET
SPRINGTIME SURPRISES ON SUNFLOWER STREET
AUTUMN DREAMS ON SUNFLOWER STREET
A CHRISTMAS TO REMEMBER ON SUNFLOWER STREET

STANDALONE STORIES
CHRISTMAS AT THE LITTLE COTTAGE BY THE SEA
THE WEDDING

Printed in Great Britain
by Amazon